BEAUTY SLEEP

A Cressida Carlisle
Psychic Detective
Mystery

HF Dobson

CONSPIRACY OF RAVENS

First published in Australia in 2024 by Conspiracy of Ravens.

Copyright © by Helen Dobson 2024

All characters and events in this publication, other than those clearly in the public domain, are fictitious and any resemblance to real persons, living or dead, is purely coincidental.

ISBN 978-0-6459145-4-2 *(digital)*

ISBN 978-0-6459145-5-9 *(paperback)*

For Nadine...

Because everyone should have a small,

loud blonde girl in their life... xx

The *Cressida Carlisle* Catalogue – the mystery history so far...

After Midnight

Beauty Sleep

Counting Sheep

Don't Let The Bedbugs Bite

Eine Kleine Nachtmusik (*coming soon!*)

Let's stay in touch!

Instagram @hfdobson

Facebook HF Dobson

"They've promised dreams can come true -

But forgot to mention that nightmares are dreams, too."

Oscar Wilde

Table of Contents

Pretty Is as Pretty does...

"You cannot be fucking serious..."

I'm muttering under my breath through clenched teeth in such a hostile manner that the words are a soft hiss.

Sorry 'bout the language, but in my defence, I'm hungry. Actually, I'm fucking starving.

Breakfast was a *very* long time ago... I've been working my ass off since 7am. One hand is reaching for the wallet in my handbag... and a warm, oozy, buttery toasted ham, cheese and avocado sandwich from Hangry cafe is so close I'm drooling like a Bloodhound...

And then my boss says those fateful words...

Kitty! There's a problem. She hates everything.

Right.

Firstly, my name is not Kitty. It's Cressida.

Cressida Carlisle.

I work at Melbourne's Florist to the Fabulous, Le Jardin. My boss, Troy James, has an army of dozens of employees and is very bad at remembering names. So he gives us all a made up one. Mine is Kitty-Kat. I have no idea why.

She is a former supermodel and wife of one of the richest men in Australia... and *everything* is the mind-blowingly vast number of floral arrangements send to her house earlier today to wish her a Happy 50th Birthday.

Of course she hates them.

How do you fill in your time when you have a handsome husband, two beautiful teenage kids (one of each, of course... Max and Ava), lovely homes everywhere, hired help to do everything and more money than you know what to do with...???

You complain.

You complain about everything.

Her name is Bo Marchesi. Her husband is top of Melbourne's power-broking food chain, Sebastian Marchesi. We call her the Boa Constrictor - and you're about to find out why...

She's mean and cold as a goddam snake.

I take a very deep breath and raise a passive-aggressive eyebrow at my boss. I think he narrows his eyes in reply, but it's difficult to tell. His tanned, handsome face of unconfirmed age has just taken a hit of Botox and is basically immobile from the cheekbones up.

You see, this was always going to happen.

Everything in Bo's world is white.

Clothes, cars, houses, interiors... and flowers. She calls it her Signature.

I call it a sad lack of imagination...

Anyone sending to Bo knows...

White Flowers.

And even if they want to send something else, we do - you guessed it - White Flowers.

However, my boss and her husband thought it'd be 'fun' to do colour for Bo's Significant Birthday.

There are many adjectives that can be applied to Bo Marchesi...

Fun not being one of them.

We're already getting smashed today. As well as doing the (very white) mountains of flowers to create a sufficiently extra experience for Bo's monster birthday bash tonight, Sunday is Mother's Day. Which in Australia, means it's the second weekend in May. We're in the fortunate position of not having to work Sunday, however tomorrow will be a marathon that begins at 4am (yes - little hand on the four...) and finishes whenever it's finally done...

Troy takes a very long, deep breath.

"Yes. I know."

I've been working here for a couple of years and I know him well enough to know that's his idea of an apology.

His eyes begin scanning the huge concrete bunker of a workroom. He raises his voice to Fearless Leader level, addressing his army of florists and junior minions.

"Anything expensive and white you don't desperately need goes to Kitty-Kat. *Now!*" as he hands me the disturbingly long list of orders that need to be redone. "Take Crepe Suzette, get this fixed and get back here soon as you can."

Grrrrrggghhh!

Yep. That's my stomach protesting violently as we wait for the monster security gates at Villa Marchesi to swing open. It's about fifteen minutes in solid inner-city traffic from the shop in busy, buzzy South Yarra, to the quiet, wide, leafy, old-money streets of Toorak.

The very stylish dark green delivery van tastefully sign written in gold is packed to the roof with white flowers. Their heady mix of sweet, exotic fragrances in such a confined space verges on sickly.

Crepe Suzette is in the passenger seat, nervous, pale and silent. Looking more like a pre-Raphaelite angel than ever, with her delicate features and waist-length blonde curls. Suzette is actually her real name. The Crepe bit is Troy's *aide memoire*. Just out of high school, she's only been with us a few months and still finds the monster mansions (and the monsters who live in them...) intimidating. I'm ten years older and this is not my first rodeo. And big houses don't intimidate me because I grew up in one. The next street, to be precise. And Toorak Dragons do not scare me, because I was raised by one. Jane Carlisle - my mum, also known as TBJ, The Beautiful Janey - is at best daunting... at worst *terrifying*.

I suspect *this* is why I get the job of wrangling the Boa Constrictor.

The pale stone tribute to a Georgian palace comes into view. Grand. Tasteful. Symmetrical. Suzette gulps. The wide stairs to the front door are covered with floral arrangements apparently too offensive to be allowed to stay in the house, making it look weirdly like somebody died there. A solitary raven waddles his fat, shiny body over to take a closer look, on the off-chance that something might be edible.

One for sorrow... right...?

Grimly I suspect what we're about to walk into will be a whole lot more painful than just sorrow...

"Lucky it's not raining, huh...?" I say softly.

It's autumn here and while the sun is reassuringly warm, there's a chill in the air. And let's face it, we're in Melbourne so rain is always a possibility. If we're careful, these arrangements - or at least the flowers - can be repurposed for other orders and not wasted.

We're barely out of the van as the huge front door is flung open. A wiry woman with dark, greying hair in a low ponytail, wearing neat black pants and matching long sleeve t-shirt appears.

"Thank God you're here!" she exclaims, her voice thick with emotion and a strong Russian accent. "I could kill her most days, but today...? Today she worse! She... - " there's a violent spluttering noise as Svetlana the Housekeeper shakes her head and throws her hands in the air, unable to find a satisfactory word in English.

Right on cue, shrieking from somewhere inside commences.

"Svetlana! SVET-LAH-NAH!!! Svetlana. NOW!!!"

Shrill, manic and ugly. Like someone yelling at a very badly behaved dog.

Svetlana glances darkly at me over the top of her glasses, mutters something under her breath that sounds like *horses's pee hole* and motions for us to come inside.

We follow her grimly through the grand and gorgeous monument to success and stealth wealth, catching glimpses of rooms as we pass by. Each one so tasteful, luxurious and immaculate it feels like we're walking through a coffee table book.

Palest French oak... white linen... huge modern canvases that look vaguely familiar and in anyone else's home could only be reproduction. Here? They're the real deal, baby.

The door to Bo's study is open. It's a beautiful, light-filled room with huge French doors that on a warmer day would be open to the sunny private courtyard bordered by hedges of glossy dark green foliage and perfect white Chanel camellias.

She's sitting with her back to the door, perched on a white Swiss ball that resembles a gigantic pearl. On the antique refectory table before her is a Mac, a pile of Happy Birthday cards and a small, white plate with a small, perfectly-cooked portion of salmon and a dainty pile of steamed Asian greens. Before Svetlana can knock, the Boa Constrictor's already upright and uptight posture stiffens.

"*That* is not ninety grams!" Without bothering to turn, she stabs a perfectly manicured neutral nail at the plate. "That is one-twenty...? One-thirty...? When I say ninety, I mean ninety. Are you trying to make me obese...?"

Still without turning she picks up the plate, presumably for Svetlana to remove.

"And don't just try to fix that one - I want a new one. No... actually I don't want that at all now. Make me one of those zero cal protein shakes."

Svetlana raises an eyebrow, possibly fantasising about smashing the plate over the Birthday Girl's head, before calmly crossing the room to retrieve it.

"And you haven't been logging Ava's macros. She's still looking chubby. We have three months til castings for Paris Fashion Week... I want her on the scales every morning."

"Mr M say she not going. Miss too much school..."

"Oh we're fucking going!" she hisses. "She's just done her first Vogue cover - I'm not losing that traction. I've rented apartments in Paris and London... hopefully she'll be booked til Christmas... I'll just pay a tutor or something..."

Svetlana's poker face is impassive. And impressive.

But if you're highly observant, you would have noticed for a split-second her eyes narrow ever so slightly.

And a muscle twitch in her cheek as her jaw clenched even tighter.

"Cressida and Suzette from Le Jardin are here to fix flowers..."

Slowly the Boa turns her gaze on us.

No matter how many times I see her, there's always that strange jolt of recognition, followed by the disconnect of seeing somebody out of context.

You see, Bo used to be a Super Model.

And I mean the real deal.

Not just a few little photo shoots and five minutes of social media fame...

I'm talking legit Super Model.

Capital S. Capital M.

International Vogue covers... Fashion Week shows... luxury ad campaigns... music videos...

Her perfect face was one of the most recognisable in the world. Growing up, her impossible cheekbones and haunting aquamarine eyes were the benchmark of beauty, glamour and success.

Those impossibly pale blue eyes are right now narrowed to mean little slits, and contorting with escalating anger, her lovely face goes from unpretty to downright ugly.

"*You!* What were you thinking...? And *what the fuck is that supposed to be???*"

That is actually one of the most gorgeous things I've ever created.

At the other end of the table is an exquisite crystal vase filled with fifty perfect roses. Entirely her husband's idea. Specially imported from South America, every spectacular bloom is the size of a tennis ball, and in every shade of pink, orange, red and yellow imaginable.

I would describe it as a gloriously indulgent, mad riot of joy because you cannot look at it without being overwhelmed by its bold, extravagant beauty.

Unless you are Her.

She stands, drawing herself up to her full imposing height. With her signature short blonde slicked back hair and white cashmere tracksuit hugging her too-thin body, she looks disturbingly like an evil henchwoman in a Bond movie.

"I come home from pilates to a house full of hideous flowers. How could you??? And as for *That!*... Fifty sick-making coloured roses! *Fifty!!!* Is this his idea of a joke...??? You know I fucking hate coloured roses! *What the fuck were you thinking...???*"

Now anyone else would be overjoyed that people had actually thought to send flowers at all...

And anyone else would be overwhelmed by such an extravagant gesture from their husband...

Not the Boa.

It's interesting how the cultivated posh vowels and soft consonants vanish, and her accent betrays her very working class beginnings when she's angry...

I begin trying to explain that her husband and Troy wanted to do something different for her Special Birthday, but it does not go well. So I cut straight to damage control.

I am, however, not saying sorry. Because none of this was my idea.

"Troy sends his apologies. We've brought a truckload of beautiful white flowers. We will fix everything."

"You can start by getting *that* out of my sight. I can't bel-"

But Round 2 of her complaining is interrupted by what sounds like the crashing roar of a dragon, and some violent swearing from a hormone-afflicted young male voice trying to control its new range of octaves.

"Oh you fuckfuckfucking piece of-"

Bo looks like she's about to implode.

"MAX MARCHESI! You have ONE DAY left!!! If you don't stop playing that fucking game and do your homework I will throw that fucking console out the window and run over it twenty times... DO NOT MAKE ME COME UP THERE!!!"

Apparently Bo's parenting tools are consequence, foul language and the threat of extreme violence.

With a little *ugh* for effort, I lift the gigantic vase and leave the room.

Svetlana sets us up on the gigantic island bench in the 'butler's pantry' - which is somewhat misleadingly named, being bigger than my entire apartment - and we get to work.

The offending plate of salmon sits by the sink. Cooked to opaque coral perfection with barely-blackened crispy skin, it smells so good it makes my stomach cry.

"You hungry?" Svetlana thrusts the plate and heavy, expensive cutlery at me. "Here! Eat! Bad to waste hundred and blahblah grams of perfectly good food..."

"Hungry...? ICYMI Max had no lunch yet... "

Max Marchesi appears in the doorway. A Mini Me of his father, one day he will be tall, dark and handsome. Right now he's figuring out how to drive what puberty, God and good genes have suddenly thrust upon him. His too-long-for-private-school dark curly hair is a wild mess. He's wearing baggy basketball shorts and a well-loved Pink Floyd t-shirt. Seeing Suzette and me, he pauses and half-raises an eyebrow (which is disarmingly sexy when his father does it... the sixteen year old version is cute and a little bit funny.)

"Yo Ladies! Didn't know we had company..."

"You have no company. You suspended! Very naughty boy! Go do homework!" Svetlana shoos him out, slapping his hand away from the giant oven door he's about to open. "And put pants on! *Please!* I know you very proud of them, but no one want to see your hairy legs..."

"How 'bout you do my Psychics for me...? I'll pay you..."

"How 'bout lazy suspended boy do his *own* physics?" Then she pauses thoughtfully, mid packing the dishwasher like a Swedish architect. "What they teaching you...?"

"Ohm's Law..." he yawns theatrically. "It's just not doin' it for me..."

"Bad dancer blames his testicles!" nods Sveta wisely.

"My *what???*" sneaking a glance down at his crotch.

I splutter a little, almost choking on the salmon and bok choi that I'm stuffing in my mouth like I've never seen food before.

"Omg! This is so good! Thank you –" Oops! I have a little attack of conscience as I remember Suzette. I offer her the teeny piece that's left. "Did you want some?"

She declines with a shy shake of her head.

Max leans on the bench and lowers his voice conspiratorially.

"Wanna know why I was suspended...?"

"No. They would not! Very busy. Trying to fix shit-show caused by your mother... What's that on your lip? You got a little-" she grabs a tea towel and heads towards his face.

"It's my moustache!" he declares proudly.

Svetlana erupts into laughter.

"*Moustache!*" she splutters, like it's the most hilarious thing she's ever heard. "Looks like little smudge of dirt! Gorky... now *that* was a moustache...."

"*So...* if I said Sveta's last comment was, in fact, a clue...?"

We shake our heads. Yes. We really should be straightening out this shit show, but who doesn't love a Bad Boy, right...?

"*So...* I hacked the Saint Nick's site and substituted *Christian* with *Communist* throughout..."

I splutter so violently I have to clamp my hand over my mouth. The thought of Melbourne's most prestigious private boys' school - the monument to power, success and capitalism... incubator for the next generation of movers and shakers - represented as socialist, let alone communist is... freaking hilarious.

"*And...* it was *weeks* before they even noticed. Only when they started getting enquiries about the free tuition for card-carrying

Party Members-" unable to finish the sentence as he dissolves into laughter.

I shake my head, giggling. As someone who was subjected to primary and secondary education at Clendon, the girl version of St Nicholas', I can just see the Powers That Be losing their tiny minds as their very proper rug is pulled from under them.

"That is *gold!* How did you not get expelled...???"

"Mr M buy school new swimming pool. And not gold. Not funny. Very naughty boy... who should be doing homework, not loitering in kitchen like stray dog."

"C'mon Svetochka! You gotta admit it's genius. Even Ladybug sent me DM...!"

"If you so *genius* why you get caught, huh...?"

"Who's Ladybug...?" as I slip the dark green Le Jardin apron over my black cashmere turtleneck and stretchy olive cargo pants, ready to start work.

The way everyone turns to look at me like I'm new here, I'm guessing I'm the only one who doesn't know.

"*OMG!* Where you been??? How can you not know..." Max shakes his head in disbelief.

"Ladybug... is a *hacker!*" Suzette is wide-eyed and awestruck.

"And *disruptor...*" Svetlana nods knowingly, sounding uncharacteristically impressed.

"And she is like totally anonymous. She is my hero." Suzette gushes, fan-girling. Big time.

Truly his father's son, Max instantly sees his way in with the pretty girl.

"Oh hell yeah! She messaged me in mer$enary!"

"How cool is the secret level with the black dragon...?" Suzette asks shyly but a little slyly.

"Man... it's killing me... No matter what I throw at it, I keep getting ganked."

"Oh... Those billboards on the freeway with just 'mercenary' - all lower caps and a dollar sign instead of a *c*...? It's a *game...*???" I'm quite pleased with my little epiphany. Clearly this is not my jam.

Suzette gives Max a sneaky Mona Lisa smile. And Young Love is great'n'all, but we really do need to hustle.

"Suzette - could you please bring in the peonies...? They should be fancy enough to replace that -" as I gesture to my mad-bright and unwanted rose bowl.

"Wouldn't you be... thirsty... after the lava caves...?" Suzette tosses the comment nonchalantly over her shoulder as she leaves the room.

He frowns, but you can see the wheels in his head turning.

"You drink the water in the well...?"

"...and you *may or may not* become invisible!" And with a theatrical *snap!* of her fingers, she disappears to the van.

Systematically we start working through every order, refurbishing or replacing, obliterating every trace of glorious colour. Just as I'm trying to wiggle a stem of tuberose into the spot vacated by a spectacular hot pink parrot tulip, the hysterical shrieking resumes.

"*Svet-lah-nah!* Where's my shake? And my supplements? I haven't eaten in four hours... *I am storing fat!*... I can *feel* myself storing fat... *Svetlana? NOW!!!!*"

Not particularly hurrying, Svetlana calmly opens a giant tub of protein powder. The label says Maximum Weight Gain. She sees me read the label, and raising an eyebrow flicks four liberal scoops into the blender with full fat milk.

"Zero Cal... I give her Zero Cal..." she mutters under her breath. "And as for starving beautiful little girl... *terrible mother!*... Beautiful husband, beautiful children... She have *everything!!!* She is terrible mother. Terrible wife. Terrible person. Horse's pee hole..."

She opens a high, out-of-the-way cupboard, pulling down a tray covered with plastic and brown glass jars of various sizes. Into a dainty white china finger bowl she deposits a cocktail of a dozen pills. Then she fishes a baking tray out of the oven and carefully arranges a dozen golden little pastries on a plate, before smothering them with tomato sauce.

"For naughty boy..." she explains to me. Fondly and a little sheepishly. "You want pirozhki...? Potato, cheese... I make! Very good!"

I glance up at the giant antique wall clock. They smell incredible, but we're seriously tight for time.

"Is okay. I pack some. You take home."

"Thank you! You are truly amazing!"

"*SVETLANA!!! WHERE THE FUCK IS MY SHAKE???*"

She sighs and raises an eyebrow at me.

"At least somebody think so..."

With a grimly satisfying whir and bang!, the van door slides and slams shut. All trace of colour obliterated and monotony restored to the Boa Constrictor's little white world, our work here is done.

Suzette's taken pics of everything we're bringing back. With so many orders in the diary for M Day tomorrow, it shouldn't be hard to find new (more appreciative) homes for all the arrangements and stray flowers. And it will make our work load a little lighter...

A text message from Troy pops up on the screen.

Unpack van and Suzette, then deliver rose vase to ChouChou.

I sigh, stuffing a pirozhki into my mouth.

If you've been wondering what Sebastian Marchesi is like, you're about to find out...

Friday 3.08pm

Accidents WILL Happen.

"Hell-ooo-ooo…?" I call out hopefully into the vast, darkened and deserted space.

Is there anything more desolate than a nightclub in the cold, hard light of day…?

No. There is not.

Technically Chou-Chou is a Gentleman's Club. The podiums and poles strategically placed amongst the tables and plush chairs give the game away. However this isn't just any titty bar. This an exclusive club where men of *very* highly disposable incomes (both legally earned and ill-gotten) come to do business and ogle the girls who work here (who are prettier, more talented and better paid than your average stripper.)

Hmmm. No cleaners. No staff.

I head towards the discreet door next to the bar which is marked 'Private'. It opens onto a corridor of identical doors - all closed except for the one furthest away which is slightly ajar. Two male voices drift out into the hallway. As I slowly and quietly walk towards it, I can make out words.

"Divorce is not an option. It'll be too expensive and she'll turn it into a media circus."

"Mmmmm. Bad for business. Bad for bank account."

"And bad for my kids..." his voice becomes impassioned.

"Then you need an *accident*..."

I stop dead in my tracks and my hand involuntarily rises to stifle the gasp that almost escapes my lips.

Seb Marchesi is about to plan the murder of his wife.

I sneak a little closer, so I don't miss anything. I can see the corner of his desk on the facing wall. Lying in front of it, with his powerful jaw resting on his elegantly crossed paws, is Nero, his Dobermann.

He sees me. His eyes light up and I know he's about to spring to his feet.

"Ssshhh!" I motion almost silently, softly holding a finger to my lips. Then I hold up two fingers. "Just give me two seconds, okay...?"

He exhales theatrically as he sinks back down to the ground.

"Are we boring you, Nero?" asks Marchesi.

"Pity she doesn't have a serious illness..." the other voice has a faint slavic accent.

"Oh she has a heart condition..."

"She has a heart...???"

Both men laugh. I stifle a giggle too. Given what that woman has put me through so far today, you really can't blame me.

"She has a heart murmur. And a dependence on phentermine and fenfluramine."

"Diet pills? Could cause a heart attack. Probably... mmmmm... yes. But can't say *when*..."

"Exactly. I can't be implicated but I need a more solid deadline. No pun intended."

They both chuckle.

"There's a new guy. Serb. Ex-military. He specialises in car accidents. The road to the beach house... on the cliffs... *very windy... very dangerous...*"

"Absolutely not. She never goes to the beach without the kids. It would need to be-"

I'm sorry but I can't listen to any more. And I'm chicken that I'm going to get busted eavesdropping. I take a deep breath and knock briskly on the doorframe.

"Mr Marchesi...? Hello...?" I call out, hoping my voice sounds chirpy and innocent.

There's a beat of silence before Nero crosses the room in a single bound and flicks the door wide open with his nose. I enter the room, with the huge vase of fifty offending roses balanced on my hip like a toddler and Nero dolphin-flicking my free hand with his muzzle, trying to make me pat him.

Seb Marchesi is reclined in the chair behind his desk. His long, muscular legs are stretched out languidly in front of him, his feet (in his very expensive shoes) rest next to his wireless keyboard.

"Ah... Miss Carlisle..." his manner is light and casual, but for a split second his eyes are dark and intense as they scan my face for any sign that I overheard something I should not have.

"My wife..." - he continues lightly, whilst looking me right in the eye - "... couldn't you just murder her...?"

I pretend to be concentrating hard on carrying the very expensive vase and flowers.

"I think I'd have to take a number..." hopefully the words sound light and jovial. "Where do you want this...?"

"Ivan, if you could take that off Miss Carlisle's hands and put it in the girls' dressing room..." his voice is smooth and authoritative.

A big guy in a very expensive black leather jacket, designer jeans and designer stubble is almost comically careful as he relieves me of the arrangement. Tanned face, immaculately barbered military-short hair and clear, piercing eyes. He'd be handsome if he didn't feel so calm and capably dangerous.

Soon as my hands are free, Nero jumps up for a pat.

"Naw!" I coo, tickling his velvety ears. "Who's a handsome boy...? *You!* Yes you are!"

"Nero. Do we need to have a chat about your Guard Dog KPIs again...?" Seb Marchesi sighs and shakes his head in mock frustration.

"I think I'm getting you in trouble..." I whisper theatrically.

"Actually..." he rearranges his lean, panther-like frame to sit straight and business-like in his chair. His dark eyes become uncharacteristically earnest. "I got you into trouble, and I need to apologise. It was bad judgement on the part of Troy and myself. You advised against it. We disregarded your counsel, then sent you in to clean up the mess. I'm sorry you were put in that situation."

I frown as I run my fingers up and down Nero's solid ribcage. I know I'm supposed to say it's okay, but you know what...? I'm actually not going to.

"I did try to tell you it was a Really Bad Idea..."

Wincing, he looks me right in the eye.

"How bad was she...?"

"Satanic. But at least I got to leave - poor Svetlana is stuck with her."

"Oh, Sveta can look after herself..." he chuckles fondly. "You know, she deliberately shrinks Bo's clothes so she thinks she's gaining weight...? Max has tried to float the theory that she's ex-KGB..."

And then he's back to business...

"Obviously I'll pay for everything - just put it on my account. And two more things..."

He opens the top drawer of his desk and pulls out an envelope addressed to Mrs S Marchesi.

"*This* is to go with Bo's Mother's Day flowers. Troy was organising a gardenia plant for delivery Sunday morning."

So when I said 'we' weren't working Sunday... when you have enough money, the rules don't apply.

"Mother's Day...? Shit! When???" Ivan has reappeared. Apparently he is scared of nothing... except the mother of his children.

"Make that *three* things..." Sebastian says with the faintest trace of a smile, placing a smooth, crisp correspondence card embossed with a bright green four-leaf clover on his desk and picking up a Montblanc pen. "*This* is to be left on the hall table of the penthouse ASAP…"

He begins writing in bold, confident cursive script.

"How much are flowers…???" Ivan has pulled the biggest roll of green hundreds I've ever seen from his pocket and proceeds to count them out to me like they're Monopoly money.

"Tasteful, not extravagant…?" I ask.

Seb looks up from his card, raising an eyebrow.

"She's young and ambitious. With competitive friends…"

"Oh. Impressive then…? Red roses, champagne and chocolates? A teddy bear, maybe…?"

"Yes! Teddy!" And the Tough Guy melts…! I delicately extract the correct number of notes from his hand. "Make it very beautiful, yes…?"

I don't know if it's a question, a threat or a warning.

With a gulp, I nod *yes* possibly a little too enthusiastically. Seb passes a blank card, envelope and pen across the desk for Ivan, then resumes putting his own card into an expensive, bright green tissue-lined envelope.

And I don't mean to - *honestly* - but I can't help but read his words…

Please don't be mad...

I will *see you tonight.*

Promise!

S xx

He seals the envelope, then turns it over to address it.

And I know exactly what he's going to write...

"Any flowers...?"

He pauses, frowning. I have a suggestion.

"How about just one of the roses...? On its own. Simple and elegant."

"Yes! Perfect. Which colour...?" he considers very seriously, like it's the most important decision he'll make today.

"There's one in graduated shades of pink... it looks like it's painted in watercolours... it's perfection..."

He smiles softly and nods.

"Perfect!" as he hands me the envelope, addressed as predicted, to Holly Golightly.

So... this is when things start getting tricky.

Holly is Sebastian Marchesi's mistress. I know *mistress* sounds a bit Continental, but it's being going on for so long *girlfriend* seems a little trivial...

Nobody knows about Holly - and nobody *can* know about Holly. Marchesi is one of the most powerful men in the country, with hints that if he went into politics he could end up running the whole show (and he'd make a very photogenic Prime Minister... which would be very novel for Australia...)

Scandal is not an option.

I'm guessing I'm one of a handful of people who know of her existence. I've been delivering notes, flowers and occasionally gift boxes (blue from Tiffany's... orange from Hermès... red from Cartier...) to the hall table of the penthouse apartment at least once a week for the past year or so. I'm guessing he trusts me with his secret because my dad is his lawyer and he figures discretion/ appreciating the gravity of the situation runs in the family.

However... even though I'm not supposed to...

I know who Holly really is!!!

And this leaves me pretty conflicted, because while I really struggle with infidelity, Holly is sweet and lovely and just thinking about her seems to make him happy. Whereas his wife is the mean-est, saddest excuse for a human being God ever put breath into...

The van sails through number plate recognition security at the service entrance of Marquis - the chic, ultra-expensive apartment tower that I'm not saying Seb Marchesi purpose-built for his mis-tress, however the timing and the location in between his family home and Chou Chou are pretty convenient. There's a private lift just for the penthouse in the corner. I punch in a six digit code, and the doors softly slide open.

Unfortunately I can't avoid my reflection on the ride up... it's completely lined with mirrors.

I screw up my nose.

Yep.

I look tired, half-assed and, like a bird with a bunch of feathers sticking out, I look ruffled.

I'm pretty unremarkable.

Not tall, not short.

Not skinny, not fat.

Longish hair that's right on the cusp of where blonde becomes brunette.

Skin that turns golden with minimal effort and isn't in too bad shape, despite my lack of interest in its welfare.

Green eyes that with more rest, more time and less apathy in the make up department can actually look quite interesting.

As suspected, the tinted moisturiser hastily slapped on at 6am has all but vanished, and most of the express attempt at mascara has relocated, raccoon-style, to my lower lids. With my one free hand I try to wipe it away, then smooth the flyaway bits from my ponytail.

The lift doors glide open onto the private entrance foyer. I key another six-digit code, and the huge, almost-black carved wood antique door clicks open.

I arrange the card and rose quickly but carefully in the delicate porcelain tray on the elegant antique hall table.

I don't have to turn it over to know that it's Hermès.

Product of an Old Money Childhood... an unusual if not especially useful skill set.

And after leaving the love letter for his mistress, I head back down to the van to make my way into the city... to help with the finishing touches for his wife's birthday party.

It's my party. And I'll be unreasonable if I want to.

I expected to walk into chaos and I am not disappointed. Or pleasantly surprised.

So… we'd finalised plans for a perfectly perfect, luxuriously glamorous fiftieth Birthday bash in one of Melbourne's prettiest restaurants on the bank of the Yarra, looking across to the twinkling city lights.

But then one month ago, the Boa Constrictor was invited to the Wedding of the Year - one thousand guests… hotel ballroom turned into Central Park… you get the picture…? - and suddenly everything is no longer *enough*. It's become an A-list party pissing competition and Bo wants to double down.

So… her husband has very fortuitously almost completed his latest addition to the Melbourne skyline - a luxury office tower. The nuts and bolts stuff is done, but no fabrics and finishes. It's a vacant, empty shell.

Or… a sensational blank canvas.

The top floor - that will be Marchesi's new corporate hq - is a vast, vacant space with floor-to-ceiling glass giving sweeping, uninterrupted views of Melbourne from the bay to the distant hills.

Every surface - walls, doors, ceiling, raw concrete floor - has been painted white for tonight. But a world of whiteness wasn't enough... so we have recreated the Left Bank (Paris...not Gaza.)

Cafe tables and chairs... planter boxes with lush shrubs and small trees... strings of light globes like the ones on the Seine cruise boats... Even the bars and food stations have been cleverly disguised as bookseller stalls.

But all of this was - you guessed it- still not *enough*.

So the *pièce de résistance*?

A carousel.

Yes.

A full size, antique, fully-functioning merry-go-round... sourced in Paris and freighted here... painted (you guessed it...) white... equipped for a DJ and a bar at the centre.

Yes.

Fully-functioning. It goes around and around, and the all white horses go up and down. We did try to point out that this was not a great idea, however the Boa was adamant.

Drunk people and revolving machinery...

What could possibly go wrong...???

Quickly I scan the state of play and automatically start calculating the Disaster Algorithm - how many workers, how much is done, how much is left and how much time remains.

With less than two hours to go, all the big stuff is done - backdrops, furniture, props. However the devil is in the details, and there's still a daunting list of tedious little finishing touches.

There's a small army of green aprons from Le Jardin attacking the carousel, tying delicate wreaths of white flowers around the horses' necks and draping pretty garlands of white flowers down every upright post. Another army of (pretty hot...!) fit young guys in Epic Events t-shirts are tweaking pieces of furniture into perfect position, or clambering up and down ladders to focus lights or wire speakers.

Now... there is one Epic Events team member that I am hoping very much will not be here. Realistically, I know that unless he's dead or hospitalised, he will have to be on this job. So let's just hope that in this swirling vortex of chaos, I see him before he sees me and I can successfully continue avoiding him. As I have for the past month...

I'm just arriving at the conclusion of Not Entirely Fucked, when Troy spots me. He's standing on the counter of the bar in the middle of the carousel, arranging a bowl of flowers that's almost as tall as he is.

"Kitty! Thank God! Get up here and give me a hand - *shoes off!!!*"

This is when I notice everyone is walking around in their socks to protect the pristine white floors - specifically the merry-go-round and the gleaming circular wooden dance floor that leads up to it.

(And thank god I chose a pair of very presentable fluffy tangerine socks this morning...)

I hustle over to Troy, unable to stop my hand from gently patting the arched neck and exquisitely chiselled fore-face of each horse I pass.

In photos, it was spectacular.

Up close, it is heartbreakingly beautiful. Each horse is unique and so finely detailed they look like they could jump from the platform and canter right out the door.

My mission is to create the matching pair to Troy's almost-finished show bowl. Pulling my secateurs and knife from my apron pocket, I get to it with machine-like efficiency, plunging the crazy-tall stems into a vase that's so big I could almost stand in it.

White heliconia… ginger lilies… gladioli… a bit of sneaky artificial wisteria that's over five feet tall to add a bit more height… and - like magic! - a jaw-dropping bowl of flowers comes to life.

"Where *is* everyone??? This needs water. Crepe Suzette? Larry?" Troy is scanning the vast room, frustration mounting in his voice.

There's still a *lot* to do… You'll know we're out of the woods when he starts singing show tunes…

The mention of Larry's name makes my eye twitch, but I daresay we'll get to that sooner rather than later.

"I'll go - I'm done here…" as I jump with not-quite catlike grace from the bar and pick up a giant watering can.

Any wall that isn't a window is completely covered with a backdrop that's a charming black and white illustration of the Parisian streetscape, so you feel like you're either on a theatre set or trapped in a weird, white comic-book alternate reality.

There's a doorway under the art nouveau-lettered Metropolitan sign… I'm guessing the fake Metro station entrance is the way to some water.

I head down the white hallway, looking for toilets or the make-shift kitchen. I get a faint whiff of food smells and I start following my nose.

And then I hear it.

Two voices fighting.

Loudly and passionately.

"You cannot be doing this! My wife could walk in here any second!!!" - his voice. Youngish, educated, authoritative. But with the unmistakeable note of panic.

"You started this! And I will *not* be ignored!" - her voice. Younger, husky, expensive. And furious.

Also (sadly) very, very familiar.

It is horrifying that they're doing this here.

It's very stupid and very, very dangerous.

I freeze, taking a very deep breath, trying to push my thudding heart back down my throat, then give the door that's in front of me a violent push to open it.

I'm guessing I'm in what will eventually be the tearoom, but right now looks like an army mess kitchen. Banks of combination ovens, bain maries and portable cooktops... trays covered with foil, giant plastic tubs filled with unidentifiable recipe components, cartons of fresh produce.

Their heads spin in unison.

Wide-eyed, alarmed and looking guilty as hell.

"I could hear you all the way down the hall! *Anybody could hear you!!!* " I hiss at them. "You need to stop this! *All of this!!!*"

I wave my free hand theatrically in the air, making it clear that I'm not just talking about the arguing. I'm talking about the whole affair.

"This is *none of your business!*" my little sister, Larry, snarls quietly at me.

"You are making it *everybody's business!!!* Anybody out there could hear you!!!" - yes. I'm repeating myself, but they don't seem to be grasping the gravity of the situation.

He inhales slowly, his too-handsome Anglo-Indian features uncharacteristically agitated.

He is Ash Knight.

Restaurateur, celebrity chef... and giant rat.

And apparently being the Groom Half of the Wedding of the Year, and a month-long Dream Honeymoon, has not been enough to make him give up his bit on the side...

My little sister.

She is a petite, pretty swirling vortex of chaos.

A high IQ, a short attention span and zero regard for consequences, she figured out far too young that when you have very big, blue eyes and the ability to make anyone laugh, the rules did not necessarily have to apply to you. My big sister, Miranda, and I have been controlling the damage from Cyclone Larry since she became capable of conscious thought.

And yes. It's a girl called Larry.

She was supposed to be a boy, so my parents started calling her Laurence in utero. Their plan failed dismally and they basically ended up with every female wile weaponised.

Right now, I am so angry with them I could bash their very attractive heads together. His wife, Angelica, is gorgeous. She is also the adored daughter of a construction magnate who is rumoured to make 'problems' disappear in the concrete foundations of skyscrapers. And my sister - despite her malfunctioning moral compass - is sweet, gorgeous and funny, and deserves so much more than to be somebody's dirty little secret.

So I thrust the watering can into her hands.

"*You!* Fill that with water and go find Troy. You are supposed to be working here, remember...??? And *You!*..." I turn on Ash, unable to think of anything polite to say to him. "You... you... *shouldn't you be cooking something?!*"

Clearly not accustomed to being shrieked at, shell-shocked, he nods vaguely at me. I'm having a bad day and I really don't need this. I start pointing accusatory fingers at everyone.

"*You* have a wife! And... *You* can do so much better than somebody else's husband!"

And I forget I'm wearing socks, so my dramatic turn to flounce out the door becomes a three-sixty degree pirouette.

When the room stops spinning, I toss my ponytail to regain my dignity and storm back into the well-ordered bedlam.

Right. Our crew is up to decorating the dozens of cafe tables with fat candles and pretty, random little vases and jars of white flowers. The Epic crew is cleaning up and bumping out, carefully re-moving every ladder, hammer, piece of rubbish and any other mun-dane little thing that will shatter our magic illusion of Wonderland. And I can faintly hear Troy singing a medley from Oklahoma!

This can only mean one thing... with barely an hour to go, we're in the home straight.

The hospitality staff have started to arrive, dressed like Paris waiters but entirely white - shirt, tie, waistcoat, pants, apron around waist, sneakers. They begin organising glasses, plates and napkins.

Furtively I scout the location of the Epic boys.

No... I can't see Him anywhere... good! I jump in and help out with the finishing touches.

And very, very quickly... we're done! Just as we're about to drag our exhausted asses to the lifts down to the carpark, Epic head hon-cho Steve calls out from the mike in the carousel's DJ booth-

"Okay! Let's fire this thing up! Everyone get on a pony!"

Everyone stops dead in their tracks and frowns slightly.

I say what everyone is thinking...

"You are not serious...???"

"Yup, Princess! I am deadly fucking serious. I need to check that this baby is fully operational with about 30 people on it. C'mon! I don't have all fucking night!"

It's almost dark outside.

With a flick of a switch, the party lights transform the strange theatre set into a fairytale. Like kids playing musical chairs, we exchange panic-stricken looks, then bolt to the carousel to snaffle a pony. The Jackson 5 start belting out of the speakers and the platform of the merry-go-round grinds into action, beginning its slow, clockwise circuit of the room.

I beat out three other people and swing my leg over to mount a spectacular jumper just as he starts rising. Another skill from the Fortunate Childhood is Pony Club, which generally doesn't come in particularly handy, however today I'll take it as a win...!

We all breathe a collective sigh of relief as the test run takes off without a hitch. Everything goes up and down, and around and around as it should.

And possibly because we're all a bit over-tired, we start singing and grooving along, enjoying the amazing experience we've created almost like the guests will.

The only thing missing is a cocktail...

And just as I'm thinking how happy and relieved I am that today is finally over, there's a smooth Irish voice so close to my ear I can feel warm breath on my cheek.

"Either I'm the unluckiest man in Melbourne or you're avoiding me..."

Oh fuck!

I'm trapped and we're not even at the chorus yet. I glance furtively up as we pass Steve. With one headphone cushion at his ear and the other arm fist-pumping the air, he seems to be living out a latent DJ fantasy... which means he's going to milk this for all remaining verses and choruses. And the funky dance break in the middle.

So... I can either hurl myself from a moving merry-go-round or face this six foot tall problem head on.

I take a deep breath, my fingers nervously tweaking the big, white grosgrain ribbon bow tying the garland on my pony-o's neck.

Then I turn to look up into brown eyes with longish, dark eye-lashes, and say one very emphatic word.

"Yes!"

He frowns slightly, but his eyes are twinkling.

"Yes to the former... or the latter...???"

"Oh the latter!... Avoiding!" I nod enthusiastically, almost having to yell to make myself heard over Michael blaming it on the boogie.

Now, you are possibly asking, what is the problem with Mister Tall, Dark and Twinkly Eyes...?

Is he unsightly?

No! Not only extremely handsome, he is also completely ripped.

Is he boring?

No! He's smart, quick-witted and capable of immense silliness.

Is he an asshole?

Also no! He is kind, thoughtful and observant.

Then what, exactly, is the problem, you ask...?

Well... about a month ago, we had a... *situation...*

In an unguarded moment, our usual inappropriate and explicit banter escalated to the proposal of a date.

To which I *may or may not* have agreed...

And I have been successfully avoiding having to deal with it ever since. Because nothing triggers my anxiety like shit getting real...

"I believe you promised me a drink... sometime..." That Irish accent - lazy, lilting and gently mocking - is highly dangerous...

"I don't believe I promised anything..." Vague and sweetly evasive - my default setting.

Though technically, I did very much promise. There was a verbal offer (on his part)... and there was verbal acceptance (on my part). Terms were vague but agreed upon... Despite taking the girl out of Law School, the Law is still strong within the girl...

"C'mon Kitty-Kat! You gonna make me ask again...?" he coaxes.

No. I am not.

I'm going to change the subject.

"How about you guys getting a carousel to the top of a fifty story building??? This is *insane!*" I enthuse loudly.

He frowns almost imperceptibly at my lack of subtlety before replying.

"Not gonna lie..." he laughs. "There was swearing, there were bruises... and there were visits to Myotherapists..."

"What's happening to it after?"

"It's going to be a fundraiser for a kid's charity. Seb Marchesi is just finalising the site."

"Oh that's a nice thing for him do!"

"That's a tax deductible thing for him to do..."

I turn, looking up at his cynical smirk and raised eyebrow, and am just about to reply in defence of my favourite mogul, when the music stops and the carousel grinds to a halt. Steve thanks us for our assistance and tells us to get the fuck out of here - literally.

Rory - despite my protests - helps me dismount my pony. He takes one last glance around the incredible fairytale we've created.

"Jesus! How can you have so much and be such a feckin miserable cow...?"

I give him a talk-to-the-hand gesture as we head for the service elevators to the carpark.

"Don't get me started! I was in the Boa's Lair all afternoon fixing the birthday deliveries she found 'offensive' - which was most of them... Seriously! Wouldn't you just be thankful people had sent you flowers at all...???"

"I know it's not very Christian, but it's difficult to argue that the world would not be a better place without Bo Marchesi..."

"I would drink to that - if I had one..." I laugh.

"Speaking of drinks... You still owe me one. How 'bout right now?"

Hmmmm. Walked right into that one!

Yes. I *do* owe him a drink. He went above and beyond to help me out when we were seriously scrambling on a job last month, and I've been successfully avoiding him ever since.

Why???

Oh not because I don't like him. Actually the contrary. I think if I got to know him better I could really, really like him. And this scares the fuck out of me.

But a deal *is* a deal so let's just get it over with.

"Sorry I can't do tonight, but-"

"A date?" he asks, maybe a little too quickly.

"Oh God no!" I shake my head at the ridiculousness of that thought. "Just playing some pool with a..."

My voice trails off, because I really don't know what to call him. *Friend* is not even close, however *annoyance* seems a little harsh.

"Hey! Are you going to the Eurovision party at Karmageddon on Sunday...? We could catch up there..."

My eye twitches at the mention of Karmageddon.

Not because it's the superstar in Ash-SuperRat-Knight's stable of hot'n'happening bars and restaurants, but because I recently posed topless for a gigantic painting for their Karma Sutra Hall of Fame. I'm sure we'll get to the story sooner or later, but let's just say there were several pitchers of cocktails involved in the decision making process.

And yes. I am going. And *shit!*. It's fancy dress and I'm supposed to have organised a costume...

As we arrive at the elevator doors that, like magic, will take us from this Parisian dream sequence and deposit us back into reality, I look up into his very symmetrical face and nod.

"Yes. I am. And yes. We can."

This comes from a place of love...

A big, therapeutic sigh of relief escapes my lips as I haul my exhausted ass up the final stairs to my fourth floor apartment.

Some people get really excited about Friday night...

These are the people who don't have to work Saturday. Some people also get really excited about Art Deco buildings. These are generally the people who don't live in them.

Yes - it's beautiful in concept.

The ceilings are high, the windows are big, the floorboards are original and the period architectural details are glorious. The reality is a tiny bathroom, an even smaller kitchen, no effective climate control, electrical circuitry ancient enough to kill you... and no goddam lift.

I'm just about to start looking for my keys in my cheeky little cherry-red hobo bag, when the front door is flung open.

It often is - you'll get used to it.

"*There you are!* Do you ever check your messages??? Is it any wonder you're single...? Here! Have a Paloma!"

A tall glass with a salted rim, filled with something frosty and apricot-coloured is thrust into my hand.

Meet Simon, my flatmate and BFF.

Imagine a giant three year-old with impeccable taste and a large disposable income. He's one of Australia's most successful and in demand fashion stylists. So as well as being the bestest Bestie a girl could wish for, he has the added benefit of a ridiculously good social calendar and is always scoring fantastic free stuff from photo shoots for my wardrobe or the house.

(*Exhibit A* - this sassy little red bag.)

I take a big slurp of perfectly chilled tequila and pink grapefruit. Simon's Perhaps-Boyfriend Danh is elegantly slumped on the couch, flicking languidly through his socials.

(*Exhibit B* - our giant ink-blue, four-seater velvet sofa.)

He glances up from his phone to say Hi and his eye twitches at my appearance. Danh is a make up artist, and when I say artist, I mean magician.

Simon comes to my rescue.

"Can I just say in her defence that she's been doing Bo Marchesi's Fiftieth...?"

"Oh man! Not just the party - I had to go to the house and redo just about every freaking Birthday order..." I growl, shaking my head as I continue self-medicating with Tequila.

"Fuck that!" says Danh calmly and quietly. "I refuse to work with her. I don't care how rich she is or how incredible her face is, she's a miserable c-"

Can't say that word in this story, Danh.

"Mmmm," Simon nods in agreement - and Simon likes *everybody*... "I did a Mummy-Daughter shoot with her for a Mother's Day edition of... oh!... something... the daughter is the sweetest, most beautiful girl ever- and it clearly don't come from *her*... she is a fucking nightmare!"

"Yeah. I did a Vogue cover with Ava... in the snow. It was freezing... she was a trooper! She's special, isn't she...? Fortunately the mother wasn't there... some crazy Russian woman brought her..."

"Svetlana. The housekeeper." I giggle. "She's good value! She's waging guerrilla warfare on Bo..."

"*Shut up!*" Simon is loving it, and is about to ask a question when that thought process gets hijacked. As it often does..."*Oh!* Carrie Rutherford's having a par-*tay* tonight. What have you got to wear?"

"Nothing! Nope. Sorry no can do. It's M-day - we're starting work at 4am. My plans involve shooting some pool then going to bed."

And even if tomorrow wasn't going to be hell, I think I'd still pass on the Influencer's Fabulous Party. I've had enough Beautiful People for one day...

"Ooooh! With Secret Agent Mick??? What are you going to wear?"

"Yes, and no idea. Probably this..." as I gesture to my black turtleneck and cargoes. "I think everything else is in the wash."

Simon throws his hands in the air and Danh shakes his head.

"Is it any wonder she's single...?! Hang on... I picked up something for you today..." as he disappears into the third bedroom, which is his office, and reappears holding up a black fluffy cardigan with a deep v neckline and pretty, sparkly jet buttons. We'll get to Mick later, but for starters let's just clarify he is *not* a Secret Agent.

(He is, however a Federal Special Agent.)

"Oh c'mon! You're killing me!" Simon's big cornflower blue eyes look pained. "Let's make an effort! We like Mick!"

"*You* like Mick. I find him irritating. However he's the only person who actually wants to play pool with me, so here we are..."

"What bra have you got on...?" as he yanks the cashmere sweater up to inspect.

Don't worry - I got used to being his Personal Barbie years ago. This morning's (very random) choice of leopard print mesh (*Exhibit C...*) receives an *Oh! That's not bad...*

He pulls the sweater over my head, ignoring my yelps as the turtleneck gets stuck on my ponytail, then slides the cardigan onto my arms *back to front.*

"Hmmph! Sexy and unexpected," Danh nods. Impressed.

"Are you sure you don't have jeans...? It would work so much better with jeans..." as he disappears into my room.

With a sigh I sink into the blue velvet and knock back my Paloma. The situation is now out of my hands.

Danh is casting sly, sidelong glances at me through his glossy black chin-length hair.

"No. No. I really can't stand it."

And in one fluid movement he places his glass on the coffee table and removes his tall, cool Vietnamese frame from the sofa to disappear into the bathroom.

There's rummaging and muttering. Then a tap runs for a few minutes. He reappears with a handful of cosmetics and a steaming face cloth.

"Close! This comes from a place of love..." he mutters softly and I shut my eyes the second before a steaming washcloth smothers my face.

Danh found his vocation at a very young age when he realised he was more interested and more proficient at hair and makeup than all of his many sisters put together. He spent years experiment-ing and perfecting his craft on them - whether they liked it or not.

With catlike grace he lowers himself to the coffee table to sit opposite me and gets to work. It's almost hypnotic having his gentle, confident fingers play with my face.

He quietly mutters instructions.

"Look up... over my left shoulder... half-close... open... duck face... fish lips..."

He reaches for his drink with a barely perceptible nod of achievement.

"Oh that's so much better!" Simon has reappeared with a pair of jeans. "What about these? Can you get into a 29...? I'm guessing you hardly ate all day...?" he asks hopefully.

"Remind me to get her mascara. This is so old it's conjunctivitis in a tube..."

Very pleasantly surprised when the zip slides up without protest, and the button does up with minimal muffin-top.

"Yay!" Simon does a little fist pump, then disappears back into my room.

"*I am not wearing the Jimmy Choo boots!*" I holler after him. *Exhibit D* - sexy as hell, but after the day I've just had, it's challenging enough staying upright as it is... "Sneakers! Please!"

Just as Simon reappears with a pair of tan suede Adidas three stripes... which I actually paid for... lol... though at a sample sale Simon got me into... my phone dings.

MICK We still on?

Corner Pocket 8.30?

I frown at the message.

"Confirmation precisely one hour before. OCD much...?"

"Hot much!" enthuses Simon. "Hey, we can drop you off - we're at a bar on Smith Street..."

"Thank you! And hot if you're a cougar maybe..."

I flick a Green Box/Tick emoji to Mick.

Danh, who had disappeared presumably to put my make up away in a perfectly ordered manner, has reappeared with a hair-brush. He points to the arm of the sofa.

"Sit!" he commands, then plucks suspiciously at the bristles of my brush. "You know you can clean this, right...?"

Yes, but I've learnt that with an OCD Fairy Godmother (make that two now...) I just leave anything icky til it makes their eye twitch - which generally doesn't take long - and it gets done for me.

Danh gets to work and... Mmmm! The satisfying feeling of someone pulling your hair almost too hard.

"Ooh! A high pony! Perfect!"

"I thought you'd want to show the back..."

Yes - it's weird being styled like you're a job, but trust me, you get used to it. And it's easier than having to think...

As we finish our drinks, I give them a blow by blow account of my day - leaving out the detour to Marchesi's penthouse.

And realising too late I also should have left out Rory...

"Oh! The hot Irish guy? With the cheeky smile and the pecs...? Oh!... OH!"

"Hot Irish guy...???" Danh is about to start asking inconvenient questions, when I'm saved by the bell... or the Uber... "Ah! Downstairs, right now Children!"

I catch my reflection as I pass the mirror over the mantelpiece and instantly feel five hundred percent better. Glowy, effortless no-makeup makeup and a smooth, sassy ponytail that shows off the low v where the cardi does up and a sneak peak of leopard bra.

I grab my giant fake fur leopard-print coat - it'll be freezing out there - and like a post-modern Melbourne Cinderella, trot down the stairs to my awaiting carriage with my two fabulous Fairy Godmothers to go smash some balls around... before turning into a pumpkin at midnight.

.

Friday 8.38pm

BItch LIves Matter

Up a side street... up like a million flights of stairs... on the top floor of a former industrial building that's over a century old, is The Corner Pocket.

Pool hall. Institution.

Formerly gritty inner-city, this one of the last bastions of Bohemian cred still standing in the now-fashionable suburb of Fitzroy. I lived just around the corner in a dodgy share-house when I was at uni and it's always been my Happy Place. Dark, cool and hushed, with a soundtrack of classic 70's rock and the soft *clink!* of balls colliding.

There's a young Greek guy behind the front counter making coffee. I smile and wave at him, passing a dozen guys waiting for a table.

"Costa! *Yassou!*"

"Hey!" he tries to look stern, but fails abysmally. "You're late! Table ten."

I make my way through the sea of green felt to our favourite table in the far corner.

It's a full house, but at this hour it's serious older guys winding down from the week with a few beers and a few frames. In a couple of hours it'll be hip young boys trying to impress pretty young girls, who generally cannot play at all. Mick's rolling the white ball around the middle pocket, watching its trajectory for any deviation from straight.

"You're late," he observes without looking up from the table.

"Yeah, yeah... So people keep saying... And you're *scared* Action Man!"

"Don't flatter yourself, Rich Girl," as he pulls a gold dollar coin from his pocket and in an impressive display of motor skills, flips it, catches it and slaps it on the back of his other hand.

"Your call - heads or tails?"

"Tails," I say, giving mine a little wiggle. "Always."

I win, and he turns to start racking up the balls.

He's wearing a chunky grey sweater and jeans that I'm pretty sure have been ironed. Even though he's not remotely my type, I can't help but notice the good shoulders, the sexy butt and the suggestion of developed quads. I'm guessing he's a little older than me, and yes, he *is*... handsome... in a conventional Action Hero kind of way.

62

I turn to dump my coat on the row of old theatre seats that surround the table.

I luxuriate in a big, full-length stretch reaching for the open rafters in the crazy-high saw-tooth ceiling. I notice two beers. One already has a smidge out of it, so I grab the other and neck it as I turn back to the table.

Mick has paused, chalk in one hand, cue in the other. Staring at me.

And I have a sneaking suspicion that even though I'm probably not remotely his type either, I've just busted him checking out *my* rear view...

He runs a hand through his sandy curls, then with one finger pushes his conservative-end-of-cool tortoiseshell glasses up his nose. He does this before almost every shot. Then he slides an easy, confident hand along the table to line up the white ball to break.

Smack! Balls go flying. Three go down.

He walks calmly around the table to line up and sink a fourth. Unable to get to any of his remaining balls, he buries the white ball to make my life as difficult as possible.

"No way to treat a lady, Action Man," I shake my head at him, reaching for his cue.

"Where's the lady...? And *no!* We're not doing this again. Get your own fucking cue!"

"I don't want to..." as I try to prise the cue out of his fingers. Seriously, with the number of people already playing, there are hardly any dodgy cues left, let alone good ones. This is why our OCD Action Man always brings his own.

With a sigh that sounds suspiciously like *for fuck's sake* he begrudgingly hands it over.

I prowl around the table, looking for a plan.

I can see a way to get the white ball out and touch one of mine, but it's going to require skill and concentration. With a bit of added luck, my ball might even find a pocket...

I bend over the table, feeling the felt under my fingertips. Left hand rocksteady, right arm raised a little higher than usual. I kiss the cue ball with the tiniest top-spin, sending it on its way to ever-so-gently knock my ball into the side pocket.

Mick applauds.

"*Shot-tah* Rich Girl!" he nods, impressed.

I do a little curtsey. Actually I'm pretty impressed with myself. I am not remotely sporty. I have zero hand-eye coordination in most situations. However, my dad and granddad take billiards *very* seriously.

We grew up with a full size table at home and this is how we bonded. With two sisters (Miranda... five years older than me... Lovely Larry... five years younger) and sometimes TBJ playing too, it made it very motivating to keep winning when losing meant going to the back of the queue. And the only way to be competitive - when everyone else was a lot taller and better practised - was to be accurate and strategic.

I get two more balls down. I can get my fourth down too, but it's going to involve reaching right across the table, standing on one foot and balancing my supporting hand on it's fingertips over one of his balls as I line up the shot. I hold my breath, just about to hit the cue ball and -

"Foul!" he calls out triumphantly.

I freeze in position, indicating that my left hand isn't even close to his ball.

"Oh not that one! The fourteen..."

I frown, looking around the table for the green and white ball. Then I realise it's underneath me.

"Seriously?! You're calling a foul with my boobs?"

"You know it! You are responsible for preventing any of your person from touching any of the object balls, Rich Girl."

"You were looking at my boobs...?"

"I didn't want to miss you touching my balls..."

"Oh. You most certainly would not want to miss me touching your balls... Trust me!"

He almost maintains his perfectly impassive cop-face, however there's a faint flicker of bemusement. When his eyes twinkle and the corners of his mouth start turning up he looks... *oh fucking hell!*... he looks cheeky and dare I say it... a bit sexy.

I hold up two fingers. Like a peace sign. Then I flip them backwards to a less polite gesture whilst mouthing the words *Two Shots* at him.

"So..." as he strolls around the table and casually pots the offending number fourteen, then pauses to consider the best way to utilise his remaining two shots to dispose of his remaining two balls, sink the black one and vanquish me... "Had any interesting dreams lately...?"

His voice is casual and his expression is neutral, but he watches for my reaction with a heightened intensity. I try to shake my head nonchalantly, but for a split second my eyes look away evasively. And unfortunately our Effective Detective didn't miss it...

Right. You're possibly wondering what's going on and who the hell is Mick anyway...

About a month ago, on the night of my twenty-seventh birthday, I started having hideous nightmares. However, it wasn't just unresolved Freudian shit - *the bad things were actually happening!*

OMG! I know, right???

Legit.

Psychic phenomena.

A girl was kidnapped and held captive for three nights. From what I saw in my dreams, I helped work out where she was and save her...

Mick was the detective who came to interview me - but (and this is where it gets weird, but Melbourne *is* a small town...) I'd already met him the night before - here, actually - playing pool.

And we've played every Friday since. Every week he's asked me the same question, and previously I've replied a straight-up No.

This week, due to the fact that my Poker Face kind of sucks, I'm going to have some explaining to do.

"Nope. No dreams!" I reply, shaking my head innocently. I haven't had any more unpleasant detective dreams and I'm not entirely unhappy to be a Psychic One Trick Pony because it was pretty stressful and traumatic.

Oh, and I potentially nearly died. There's also that...

And it's looking almost convincing, until my eyes can no longer hold his gaze and slide downwards.

"What?" as he straightens to give me his undivided attention.

"Technically not a dream... I just kinda overheard something..."

"Technically, physical evidence is more compelling to me than whatever's lurks in your sub-conscious. So...?"

I shake my head, as the ramifications start unravelling. Bad things. Very Bad Things.

He rests his cue against the table and sinking into the seat right next to where I'm standing, picks up his beer and takes a long swig.

"I'm not hitting another ball until you tell me what's going on."

With a heavy sigh, I collapse into the seat next to him and stare down at the elaborately patterned (and highly questionable, somewhat sticky) antique carpet. As the hashtag #bitchlivesmatter flashes through my head, I take a very deep breath before blurting out -

"I heard Seb Marchesi talking about getting rid of his wife."

He stares long and hard into my face.

Up close his eyes are every colour of the ocean. Around the corners of his mouth, he has slightly darker stripes in his scruffy, sandy two-day growth. He has a crescent-shaped scar on his cheek that's only visible when the light catches it in a certain way.

He raises an eyebrow and chuckles drolly.

"I had to interview her once. Can't say I'd blame him... When...? Where'd the convo take place...? Who was he talking to...?"

"This afternoon at ChouChou. He was in the office with his right-hand man. Big Croatian dude."

"Ivan Vidovic....? Now *there's* an interesting CV for you... What were you doing at ChouChou?" Mick frowns at me.

"Getting the card for his Mother's Day delivery to Bo... ironically..."

"Tell me. Word for word."

And I relate the eavesdropped conversation as accurately as I can remember... leaving out the bit about the penthouse.

"But why does he want her gone? Aren't they like the Perfect Family? Isn't he very happily married?"

I shift uncomfortably in my seat, then knock back some beer. Very deliberately *not* looking at him, yet I can feel his eyes on me. Intently. His instinct is too good and he's getting to know me a little too well. He knows he's onto something.

I take a very deep breath, hoping I can start this without having to finish it.

"So... imagine a Venn diagram... He is very happy, and very married... but the two circles do not necessarily overlap..."

"So he's having an affair..." he replies without missing a beat.

"I didn't say that..."

"You didn't have to. With who?"

"I don't know"

"Yes you do. He'd send flowers. Who is she?"

Fuck!Fuck!Fuck! If there's potentially anything worse than telling the biggest secret of the most powerful man in Australia to a Federal Agent, I can't think of it right now... How the fuck do I get myself out of this?

Boom! A little flash of inspiration. Plausible. Not *entirely* lying - and with enough truth to make it convincing.

"We sometimes deliver to him at ChouChou. And they're not for Bo - not her style. Maybe it's one of the girls who works there...?"

"That's hardly *his* style." He narrows his eyes suspiciously. "Are you sure you don't have a name for me?"

"Nope. And if I did, I couldn't tell you. There's no exact word for it, but it's like Client Privilege."

"I have a very exact word for you - *withholding*. And you know it's a criminal offence."

Yes. I do know. Coming from a family of Queen Street lawyers and unceremoniously ditching a law degree just before I was supposed to graduate...

"I do! I could write a few thousand words on withholding, if you like." I smile sweetly, hoping this attempt at a subject change will work.

He's about to say something, when his face softens and he almost smiles.

"You have your grandmother's eyes..."

Yes I do - and thank you Delia Carlisle, for the uncommonly very green eyes... and also to Danh for making them look extra fetching.

And yes. He also knows my Gran.

(Melbourne. Small town. Remember...?)

Gran - as well as being my favourite person on the planet - is psychic. Like seriously talented. As well as being on celebrity's speed dials, she sometimes gets called in to help police with enquiries.

Which is how she met Mick...

They somehow bonded and he's taken to hanging with her, helping with all the stuff around their too-big house that my Grand-dad shouldn't be attempting at his age. Gran is also on the Give Mick A Chance Team and has been trying to set us up for months.

"I wish I could see like she does," I chuckle ruefully. "I'd be a whole lot more useful and it'd be a whole lot less traumatic..."

"You will. With practice. And experience. She's got about fifty years on you..."

And I don't know what makes me more uncomfortable - discussing my reluctant super-power or Mick being nice to me - however there's clearly only one thing to do.

Change the subject.

"So... are you going to finish this off so I can demand a re-match... or are you going to sit there staring at me?"

"With pleasure, Rich Girl. Best of five...?"

However, he had me very convincingly beaten in three. Exhausted, distracted and unhappy with myself for spilling Seb's beans, I got my ass whooped.

On the bright side, I managed to get at least one down each game, so my naked butt was not required to make a surprise cameo... (*Huh?* you ask...? Quaint Australian custom called The Pants Rule. Failing to sink a ball before your opponent sinks the black means you have to run around the table with your pants down. *I kid you not!*)

It's not even ten pm when his white ute monster-truck (that's what we call a 'pick up'...) pulls up out the front of my apartment building.

He insists on driving me home and he insists on walking me up to my door. I found out the first week trying to argue that neither was necessary is useless.

And it saves me from having to pay for an Uber...

Just as we're about to get out of the car, he turns thoughtfully to me.

"If you happened to have any dreams about the Melbourne Cup, it'd be extremely helpful..."

"It's not Netflix, Action Man. I can't just login in and find out who wins a horse race..."

Like... *seriously...?*

He lets out an exasperated sigh.

"Not that... There's been chatter... terrorist activity...damage, disruption... something really big... We're six months out, so *anything* that can get us barking up the right tree..."

I shudder involuntarily.

We do a lot of jobs at Flemington racecourse. The thought of 80,000 people and all those beautiful horses under attack is sickening. I promise him if I see anything Spring Racing Carnival that I'll let him know.

We climb all those stairs - he does it with ease.

Me not so much. I fish my keys out of my pocket and they clatter to the ground.

"Ouch!"

We both bend to pick them up and crash our heads together.

"Are you okay?" he grabs my hands to steady me.

"Ouch!" I yelp again as a spark of electricity shocks me. Not the first time this has happened... "Could you stop doing that?"

"Once again, how do you know it's me and not you...?"

Shaking my head, I open the front door.

"We're going to have to resume this charming banter next week because I'm starting work at four tomorrow morning-"

"*Four!* What the...?"

"Mother's Day. We're not working Sunday so-"

"Hey - can you make some flowers for me? I'm driving down to see Mum after work... I can pick them up on the way through..."

"Only God can make flowers - oh! and a few crazy Dutch horticultural geneticists - but sure, I can put something together for you. How much you wanna spend?"

He looks nervous and bewildered - the way most men look when it comes to buying flowers. I come to his rescue.

"Special but not ridiculous? About 150."

He looks a bit shocked - the way most men do when they find out how much flowers cost.

"Errrr... okay..."

"What colours does she like? Pastel? Bright? Pretty? She's a Gardener, right...?" I know this because Mick's given my gran iris bulbs from her garden.

"She loves her garden!" he smiles, "...and she loves purple and blue things because they're good for the bees."

I make a quick note on my phone - *Mother of Mick - blue/purple, interesting/pretty, wet-packed for travel, $150.*

"Shouldn't you be getting home to Candy...?" I ask sweetly.

I've never met her, but from the way Mick talks about her, she sounds like a Hard Work Princess.

"Hmmm..." he mutters grimly. "It's not even late, but there'll probably be payback..."

Then I thank him for the ride, wave good night and trot off to bed... and after booking a ride for seriously stupid-o-clock, I set an alarm that has the little hand on the *three* (!) and wriggle into bed... hoping that I'll fall asleep *pronto!* because there sadly aren't a whole lot of hours before I have to get up again...

You can see soft, black leather gloves on a black leather steering wheel... at the centre of which the words Aston Martin have been placed on a pair of wings.

It's dark and a little foggy outside. Visibility is minimal - the headlights aren't as bright as they should be. You can just make out an embankment to your left. To your right is a dark void. Within and without the car, there is complete silence.

Without indicating the vehicle turns right and drives up what seems to be a laneway.

It opens out into a small flat, open space. Tyres crunch on raw gravel. The interior has a sense of luxe spaciousness and it feels like you're sitting up quite high...

We're in an Aston SUV...

We're in Seb Marchesi's town car!!!

From the far corner headlights flash twice.

As you get close, a hand appears from the driver window and motions the Aston to approach.

We pull up alongside the open window.

From the dark interior comes a voice.

Calm. Quiet. Foreign.

"Tomorrow night. As discussed. Yes?"

Yes. You can't see the driver, but silently they give confirmation.

"The white Porsche. Yes?"

Yes.

OMG! Bo's car...???

"You have my money?"

A bulging envelope is silently handed out the window.

"Half now. Half later. Do not contact me. I contact you."

A burner phone is tossed into the car, landing with a gentle *thud* in the driver's lap.

As the window glides up, the unremarkable black Range Rover pulls away from you and disappears into the night...

The huge, almost-black antique door clicks softly closed. Seb Marchesi walks quietly through the entrance foyer of his secret penthouse. French jazz plays softly from an invisible sound system. The living room is dimly lit.

Across the river, the city skyline rises magnificently (if a little incongruously) from the surrounding parkland. The distant lights twinkle, soft-focussed in the fog.

At first glance, the room appears empty.

Then on the coffee table you notice a big, expensive, crystal wine glass, with an elegant few mouthfuls of pinot remaining and a delicately scented candle burnt to entirely molten wax.

As you approach the oversize café au lait linen modular sofa, you notice a bare foot on the edge of the chaise. Pretty... pedicured with ballerina pink toenails.

Navy silk men's pyjamas.

Her other foot is tucked up underneath her. Curled up in a child-like ball, her soft, smooth cheek rests on her hand and her glossy dark hair falls a little over her face, gleaming in the half-light.

Meet Holly.

Sebastian Marchesi stands, staring at her for what seems like a very long time. He frowns slightly, shaking his head. His jaw clenches. He swallows hard.

He loses the fight with his emotions.

He sinks to his knees and gently kisses her instep.

"I'm so sorry," he shakes his head and whispers it again, "I'm so sorry. You deserve better than this."

Uncertain which is more disconcerting... Sebastian Marchesi breaking down or Sebastian Marchesi apologising. Twice.

Holly stirs, stretching like a cat. Her eyes blink lazily open.

"Hey you!" she whispers huskily, before focussing on his very white ensemble. With a lazy grin, she softly starts singing the chorus to *Night Fever*.

"Baby, I'm sorry..." his fingertips trace her skin from her foot to her elegant ankle. His hand gently clasps her slim calf. Like he never wants to let it go. "Bo lost an earring and we had to turn the place upside down-"

"Shhhhh!" she reaches down and softly touches a finger to his lips. "It doesn't matter. I know what I signed up for... You're here now."

He shakes his head in amazed wonder at how beautiful she is, then reaches to pick up a paperback that's fallen from her dozing fingertips to the floor.

"This isn't good enough. You deserve better."

"Better than Amor Towles...??? That bar is pretty high..." she raises a perfectly arched eyebrow at him.

"You know what I mean... And do we need to buy you pyjamas...?" he leans forward to straighten the collar.

"I like yours. They smell like you..." she counters, her voice light and musical. Almost child-like.

Unable to stay away from her for any longer, he kicks off his shoes and climbs up next to her on the chaise.

Their bodies draw to each other like magnets. She buries her pretty face in his neck and inhales him. He wraps his strong arms around her slim shoulders and pulls her into his chest. His heart feels like it might burst.

The smell of her hair... of her skin... of *her* intoxicates him. Her weight anchors him... makes him feel safe and calm.

He sets an alarm on his watch and pulling her closer, gently kisses the top of her head.

"I love you," she whispers so softly only his ears could hear it.

"And I love you, my darling," he whispers back.

And they drift off to sleep in each others' arms...

The soft chimes of an alarm...

He rolls away from her, so careful not to wake her.

He goes to the bedroom and pulls back the soft, fluffy quilt. He wishes with all his heart he could slide into the crisp, fresh sheets with Holly and never leave.

The chimes continue.

He goes back to the sofa and scoops her up in his arms like a child. Carefully he puts her to bed, pulling the covers over her. He knows he must go, yet he pauses to watch her sleep... feeling her soft breath on the pillow...

The chimes start getting louder.

Gently pushes a strand of hair from her brow, then bends down to kiss her forehead. From somewhere in her dreams, Holly smiles.

The chimes are now so loud it's almost unpleasant and suddenly... whoah!... you're in the chaotic, clashing bright Bollywood fantasy that is Karmageddon.

You're in the corridor that leads to the restrooms, kitchen and fire escape. Ahead of you, you can just make out Sebastian Marchesi carrying Holly...

Oh God! The chimes!!! Make them stop!

Then you notice the larger than life portrait of yourself. Naked. Hanging upside down off the bed with the soles of your feet on Tex's naked chest.

They promised they wouldn't use your face!

Everyone's going to know it's you...

What the fuck are you going to do??? This is a disaster... And then you realise it's not quite right... He's a little shorter and a lot narrower than Seb Marchesi. He's wearing a black hoodie.

The chimes are so loud they're almost deafening.

I'm trying to think... trying to make sense... but I can't...

They're too loud...

And it's not Holly... it's too small to be Holly... but it's somehow familiar...

Omg! It's Larry!

Limp in his arms like a rag doll.

He's got Larry!!!

I try to scream her name, but nothing comes out.

I try to run, but my legs don't go forward.

He disappears through the door of the fire escape stair well, taking Larry with him.

And he must be going down, because why would he go up...?

Why would he go up?

Why would he go up?

And the chimes!

The chimes do not stop.

Saturday 3.22am

Welcome to my nightmares...

With a spluttering gasp, I drag myself back into my bedroom.

My heart is in my throat and my pulse is thudding in my ears. In the darkness I hang onto the bed to stop it spinning, wishing that fucking alarm would just stop...

Oh shit!

That would be *my* alarm. And the relief of escaping my nightmare is replaced by the fresh hell of the realisation that I need to be vertical and functioning. Pretty much immediately.

I hit the lamp on my bedside table, swearing and shuddering as the bright light nearly blinds me.

I throw my legs out of the bed.

They hit the ground, feeling like jelly.

Crap! As if seeing weird demons in your head isn't bad enough, you also get to feel like you're going to die...

Apparently this a gift.

I drag my sad body to our tiny, freezing, white-tiled bathroom and spin the taps to full blast. Thanks to the giant power-shower head Simon installed, the pressure pounding my head is almost strong enough to make me forget everything I've just seen.

Almost.

My Uber drops me in the bluestone laneway behind Le Jardin. Living so close to work is extremely handy and not entirely an accident. Usually I just walk. Ordinarily, it's a very pleasant ten-ish minute stroll through the bougie tree-lined streets of glamorous South Yarra. Starting at 4am however, is neither 'ordinary' nor pleasant.

The giant steel sliding door to the concrete bunker workroom is open. Like a small army of undead, we drag our not entirely functioning selves past the sea of giant buckets of flowers and into the overly bright fluorescent light. We throw our coats and handbags under the gigantic workbench that almost fills the entire space and take our places at it.

I inhale very slowly.

Like Valentine's Day, Mother's Day is so insanely, ridiculously busy, just thinking about it can make you start spiralling.

However...

You start.

You keep on going.

And eventually you will finish.

I repeat this to myself three times before picking up the top order from the pile waiting on my work station. They already will have been sorted into priority - I just have to remember to do something for Mick's mum before all the really special, interesting stuff gets taken.

Despite the ungodly hour, our fearless leader Troy looks tall, tanned and glamorous as ever.

His three favourite things - beauty, adrenaline and making money. He lives for this. From his position at the top of the work-bench, he is simultaneously discussing the day with Libby (the ring-master who keeps this circus on track, making sure the orders get done, the egos stay in check and the customers stay happy), keeping a watchful eye on his twenty plus employees in the workroom and deftly thrusting tall, fat yellow roses into a pretty painted ceramic pot. My station is right next to him.

This is not always a good thing.

He pauses, looking around frowning.

"Where's Larry?"

I shake my head, and suddenly find plucking the pollen from some lily stamens requires all my attention. When it's crazy-busy Troy gets in a few extra casuals do all the low-skill stuff - sweeping floors, making tea, getting food - to save precious minutes. However

I'm struggling to see *dogsbody* fitting in with Lovely Larry's best version of herself.

"Kitty Kat! Where the fuck is she…?"

I hold up a talk-to-the-hand palm.

"Did anyone ask me and did I say it was a good idea…? Nope. And nope."

"But Janey said she'd worked in your father's office!"

"For forty-three minutes. She turned up, arranged the stationery on her desk, went out to get coffee and never came back."

True story.

"You!" he points to an attractive and bewildered young man who's attempting to sweep away the already growing sea of discarded foliage on the floor. "I would like a cup of tea, precisely the colour of a gingernut snap, with ten grains of sugar. Not nine. Not eleven. Gottit…?"

And he *will know the difference.*

Trust me.

I've only been working here a few years, and I know there's a couple of noses out of joint that I became Troy's righthand girl without 'serving my apprenticeship'.

But you know what? I am *really* good at my job.

I'm fast, I have excellent attention to detail, I try hard to make people happy and I'm really passionate about flowers.

A couple of hours in and I've already smashed out a dozen orders. I feel I'm sufficiently ahead to go find some flowers for Mother of Mick.

I stick my head into the huge, walk-in cool room in case there's some forgotten treasure hiding. It's a couple of degrees warmer than your standard fridge - and sadly not a whole lot warmer than it is outside. Flowers *really* do not like artificial heat, so our work environment has absolutely no heating. You kind of get used to it, but you never learn to like it...

Hmmm... no joy.

I do a lap, beginning at the delivery bay down the back. Dozens of giant buckets of flowers from suppliers, still waiting for Junior Minions to unwrap them, clean them up, trim them and make them look suitably fancy for the shop. Anything interesting is sadly the wrong colour...

I make my way out to the shop, which could not be more glamorous if it tried. Dark marble, mirrors and soft lighting make the overwhelming display of flowers the hero.

Bingo!

Delphinium, calla lilies, tulips, a few feature plush blue roses… and some dark, glossy camellia foliage to finish… Hmmmm… ornamental kale??? Could she be a little bit kooky…? I'm going with *yes!*

It's still dark outside and the usually lively shopping strip is deserted. I cast a wistful last glance out at the world, for a second wishing I was sleeping in and about to start my lazy weekend.

"Meh!… Meh!…"

All I can see is a chunky black tail feather pointed to the sky, balanced precariously on the edge of a rubbish bin in the street. The rest of the raven appears with a beakful of fast food packaging, which he flings away in disgust and goes diving again.

Meh indeed.

And not distracted by the pressure of work for a second, my mind goes back…

The black Range Rover… the envelope… Holly… Karmageddon… Larry…

I shudder.

It's just a dream, right…?

So why do you feel weird and sick…?

"Kitty Kat! Where are you??? Food! Now!"

With my armload of gorgeous purple and blue, I return to the workroom. Platters of pastries and hot breakfast sandwiches have appeared. Junior minions are distributing coffees, fervently hoping that Hangry cafe has got the order right.

Food! That's why I feel off! *I'm hungry!*

I grab an egg'n'bacon brioche and take a bite.

Yummy!

While Troy pauses to pick at an apricot danish, he flicks through his photos from the party last night. We are just the hired help. He always scores an invite.

"Oh it was *fabulous!*" he enthuses, "Ava looked *divine...* such a gorgeous girl! And the Boa looked *incredible* in a white YSL Le Smoking with *nothing underneath it!...* Such a fun night - oh! Until she lost her fucking Paspaley earring and we had to turn the whole fucking place upside down looking for it..."

Say what...???

No. No. No. No. No.

Fuck!

A crashing wave of nausea, followed by slow but very steadily rising panic.

So it's not just a dream...

Here we go again...

It's for real.

Crap.

However, whilst bitch lives *do* matter, I have to pretend none of it's my problem for now because today needs my undivided attention.

As well as M-Day, there's also all the usual matches, hatches and despatches...

So I'll be able to avoid thoughts of hitmen and kidnappers. For a little while, anyway...

It's a little after 9am when Lovely Larry finally graces us with her presence... resplendent in an oversize fluffy pink sweater masquerading as a dress, crochet tights and ankle boots. Her golden ombre locks are twisted up into a French roll.

"What the fuck are you wearing???"

"I thought it said 'Mother's Day'!"

"When it actually says 'I forgot my pants'..."

Her eyes flick over my hastily chucked on ensemble.

Black oversize jumper. Black leggings. Chocolate apres-ski boots with fake fur cuffs. (I told you it's cold in here, right...?) Orange, yellow and red argyle scarf.

She raises her Very Expensive eyebrows at me.

"Pot. Kettle. Black."

Hard to argue that she does not have a point...

Troy appears, clearly not happy that he has just had to make his own cup of tea, and starts barking at her.

"What time do you call this??? You were supposed to start at *four*!"

Larry blinks in beautiful, wide-eyed disbelief.

"You were serious about that...? I thought it was a joke... like... *really*... 4am is just ludicrous..."

"You can start by sweeping the floor-"

"Hmmmm... is there something else? That doesn't really work for me..."

Troy is staring at Larry like she's from another planet, unsure whether to completely lose his shit or start laughing.

"Maybe I could have a go at something like that..." as she gestures to the spectacular show bowl Troy's working on. Crazy bright colours and bold shapes, it treads the very fine line of kooky yet still sophisticated and beautiful. It's for Maud the eccentric fashion designer from her son, and there's probably only about a dozen florists in the world with the talent to pull it off.

Troy stands staring at her, magenta zinnia in one hand, knife in the other.

"Hmmmm... maybe I'll just go home and have a nap. I'm not feeling the vibe in here..."

Troy turns to stare at me in disbelief.

"Not my idea. Not my circus. Not my ponies."

The next few hours pass in a blur of flowers and orders, punctuated with very regular arrivals of carbs. I don't know whether Troy really wants to look after us, or accepts that there's a direct correlation between output and blood sugar levels.

I have a dainty white hyacinth posy almost finished in one hand (a 'thank you' to the Boa Constrictor for the swell party last night...) and a gigantic piece of Black Forest Cake in the other, when Ruby (not her real name) the Shop Girl appears next to me.

"There's a guy to see you."

The entire workroom turns and cranes their heads like meerkats.

Troy tries to raise a *really?* eyebrow but the botox wins.

"Not Seb Marchesi...?"

"Nope. Younger. Cooler."

I frown, shaking my head. I got nothing.

I walk out to the shop, with Troy hot on my heels. In here, everybody has a very unhealthy interest in everyone else's social lives.

Danh is standing there in black puffer jacket and jeans, perfectly still but with his eyes constantly prowling over the displays, the walls, the ceiling, the floor. Equal parts bored and uncomfortable.

"Oh Jesus!" he mutters at me, holding up a hand to shield his eyes. "Do you try to look bad...???"

I stuff the rest of the cake in my mouth and grunt an unintelligible greeting to him. I'd like to say I'm beyond the point of caring, but I don't think there was any danger of me getting anywhere near caring this morning...

"I need some Singapore orchids for my mother."

"Really...? That's such an Asian cliché..."

"Asian cliché??? If she was here, she'd take one look at your hands and say *ohlovetha'whyyounoguhboy-frehnd...*"

Troy and I stifle giggles, not wanting to be un-PC.

"Oh it's okay. It's only racist when *you* impersonate my Vietnamese nail bar mother. When I do it, it's fucking hilarious."

Good to know...

"Okay... so the orchid is not-negotiable, but I think we can do better..." I hold up a purple phalaenopsis plant growing hydroponically in a cool glass vase. "See! Much, much better!"

He nods. Impressed.

Ruby sits him down at the desk to write a card, and I disappear back to the bunker to continue saving the world... one Floral Emergency at a time...

I've barely picked up Bo's Thank You posy when Ruby reappears at my shoulder.

"There's a child in the shop. For you."

A *what..?*

A bit bemused but more pissed off, because now I'm getting behind schedule, I follow her out into the marble'n'mirror theatre of flowers.

And there stands a barely teenage girl, with the endearing awkwardness of a baby gazelle but more lovely than any flower in the room. Long, straight glossy dark hair… pale olive skin… and the palest, most incredible aquamarine eyes…

Just like her mother.

Meet Ava Marchesi.

"Cressida…?" she asks with sweet uncertainty.

"Hey Ava… Watcha doin'…?"

She thrusts her hands inside the pouch of her hoodie, looking a little guilt-struck.

"I'm supposed to be having a cryosauna…"

"What the hell is that…?"

"It freezes your fat cells and gets rid of cellulite."

"I'm pretty sure you don't either," I smile at her.

"Oh but I do!" she protests, wide-eyed and earnest. "Mum took a photo of the back of my thighs…"

I try not to frown as Sveta's words echo in my head…

Terrible mother… terrible mother

"Did you need some flowers?"

She hands me a crisp, white little envelope… addressed to Mummy.

I nod.

"For tomorrow…? Got it! I'll put it on your Dad's account."

"Oh no! I can pay. I've done a few jobs..." as she pulls a bunch of hundred dollar bills from the pocket of her tiny jeans.

"Looks like your parents pay better than mine did for walking the dog..."

She giggles self-consciously.

"Modelling jobs," she explains quietly. Embarrassed.

"Nice work if you can get it!"

Every little girls' dream, right...? But from the increasingly uncomfortable look on her face, apparently not this one.

"It makes Mum happy..."

"But what would make you happy...?"

She looks at me, almost shocked.

And as someone who spent far too long trying to please everyone by doing what my pedigree said I should be good at, rather than what made my heart happy, I can see this is a question Ava never gets asked.

"I want to go to America."

"To model...?"

"Oh God no! I want to go to Harvard and get my MBA. Then I want to be Dad's CFO..." she replies quietly, but with awe-inspiring determination.

Can't help it - my jaw drops open.

Not the answer we were expecting, right...???

"Not that he needs a Secret Weapon, but you'd be *dangerous!* You go Girl!"

Ava rewards my comment with an almost smug Mona Lisa smile.

"I know, right...? Hey! Do I tell you what I'd like to send her?"

I nod, impressed anyone that young would have an opinion.

"Iceberg roses... with... what are those?" pointing at a vase of little green berries that look like holly gone wrong.

"Hypericum perforatum. Commonly called St John's Wort. Good choice! You have impeccable taste."

She smiles, surprised and relieved. You kinda get the feeling she doesn't get validated nearly enough.

I fish one note out of her hands.

"Enjoy your cryosauna!" I call after her as she heads for the door.

She glances back over her shoulder, raising a perfectly arched eyebrow.

"I'm about stand naked in a tank that's minus one-twenty degrees... One does not *enjoy* the cryosauna..."

And for a beautiful minute, I look at her and instead of the mother, only see her very charming and disarming father.

More hours pass... more orders... more salt/fat/sugar and bad carbs... more cheeky banter from the workroom...

As we cross the line from Over-Tired into Exhaustion, everything is suddenly ridiculously funny.

I slip out to the shop in search of one very gorgeous thing to be the focal point of an arranged bunch of brighter pastel shades for someone's nanna.

It's getting late in the day, and even though we started with an incomprehensibly epic amount of stock, the shop is rapidly approaching empty.

Just as I'm about to start truly despairing...

Bingo! Disco-pink disbud chrysanthemums! I'm about to fish an absolutely perfect big, fluffy globe of petals from its vase when a black Aston Martin SUV prowls to a stop at the shop's front door.

My brain jolts me back to last night.

My breath catches in my throat and a wave of panic crashes over me.

The man who just last night threw his wife a lavish 50th Birth-day... then met with a hitman to pay for her execution... then fell asleep in the arms of his mistress... is about to walk through the door.

In my haste to vanish out the back, I almost crash straight into a geeky student-type guy waiting to buy a bunch of variegated hot pink and white tulips.

Almost instantaneously Ruby is following behind me.

"Seb Marchesi needs to see you urgently. Says it's a matter of life or death."

Interesting choice of words.

"Hands up who's happy the Marchesi's are Kitty-Kat's prob-lem...?" Troy asks jubilantly.

Every florist in the workroom enthusiastically raises whatever hand they have free.

Muttering *fuckers!* under my breath, I drag my reluctant ass out to the shop for my date with the devil.

Tall, dark, handsome and in weekend (designer) casual mode, he flings both hands out in a theatrical manner.

"Where are all the flowers...???"

"Mother's Day. You're about eleven hours too late." I know I should probably sugar-coat it, but I'm trying to stop myself from staring at his hands - the hands that handed the envelope to the hitman... the hands that carried Holly to bed...

I'm trying to keep my breathing calm and my gaze neutral, but being close to him sends a bolt of electricity to my heart and makes my skin prickle.

This is how I know it wasn't just a dream.

And this means it's going to be up to me to fix it.

"Surely there's something out the back...?" he cajoles hopefully.

He's really not used to hearing No, is he...? And I know he's usually my favourite client, but right now I'm not particularly disposed to be doing him any favours.

I shake my head.

"We're closing soon. If we've ordered right, everything *should* be gone by now..."

And then he notices geeky boy about to leave with his fancy gift-wrapped tulips.

"Hello! I'm Sebastian - who are you...?" smiling, commencing his charm offensive.

"Jordyn. With a *y*..."

"Well, Jordyn-With-A-Why, it appears I've left my run a little late... How much did you pay for those...?" as he gestures to the tulips.

"One hundred." Jordyn answers warily.

"I'll give you four hundred for them..." as he pulls a pile of smooth, bright green hundred dollar bills from a black crocodile wallet.

A hard, unattractive light suddenly flickers in Geek-boy's eyes.

"You can have them for seven fifty."

Sebastian Marchesi laughs out loud.

Jordyn is clearly unsure if this is a good thing or a bad thing.

"Ah, Jordyn-With-A-Why, never mistake recklessness for stupidity... and always know when to take the money..." and with a fond pat on Jordyn's back, he turns and starts walking out the door.

"Five hundred!" Jordyn calls after him.

Seb ignores him.

"Okay. Four."

Seb shakes his head a little, keeping on walking.

"Three...?" Jordyn sees it slipping through his fingers and starts panicking. Seb is almost out the door.

"Okay. Two hundred."

And Seb turns, with two bright green hundred dollar notes already in his hand. With clear misgivings, Jordyn hands over the tulips and snatches the cash.

Seb frowns slightly. Concerned.

"Don't dwell on Could Have Been…" clasping Jordyn's elbow in a kind, fatherly way. "You still doubled your money in three minutes. I'd take that as a win, yes…?"

Jordyn appears to think it over, then nods slowly in agreement before leaving.

Seb holds up his tulips triumphantly.

"Problem solved!"

At this point, I've been working for 12 hours straight and have consumed enough sugar to visually represent a diabetic coma. I am physically and mentally shredded.

I shake my head at him, trying to work out if he's just behaved like an asshole or not, and trying to *not* think about the homicidal solution to his Other Problem…

Trying to stop the loop going round and round my exhausted brain…

He's going to kill his wife tonight... but she's a real bitch... but her life still matters, right?... but we really like Seb... but he's going to kill his wife tonight...

Suddenly Nero pops up in the passenger seat of the Aston, a plush baby pink dragon held carefully in his powerful jaws.

Can't help it... I giggle.

"Ah yes... my fearless chief of security and his assistant, Gary..." raising an eyebrow, he shakes his head.

"*Gary???*" Despite myself, I engage. Just when you thought nothing could be funnier than a Dobermann with a pink teddy...

"Sveta gave it to Ava for her birthday. Zmey Gorynych was a bit much for ten year old, so she called it Gary. Nero kept stealing it - no matter where Ava hid it - and now Find Gary! is their favourite game."

Realising we're talking about him, he sits up very straight, doing a super-cute sideways head-tilt.

"Who was standing in the middle of my billiard table this morning trying to rescue Gary from the top of the light shade, hmmmm...?"

Is it just me, or is it virtually impossible to remain aloof from this man...?

Nero looks away, evasively.

"I know you love her, but that Ava will get you into trouble! Pretty girls are always trouble..." laughing and shaking his head, he turns to go. "And on that note... Enjoy your weekend... hope you get out of here soon - all work, no play, yada yada...."

How can someone about to kill their wife be so goddam charming?

And my time for avoiding thinking about all that is rapidly running out.

What the hell am I supposed to do about it...?

Back at the bench, I grab a towel and wipe down my work station, flicking bits of stem, foliage and other crap onto the floor for a junior to sweep up.

Reach for my next order and... *there's nothing there!* Omfg! We're finally done! Everyone is starting to help Ruby the Shop Girl bring the few remaining vases into the cool room to keep them happy til Monday, and I start on my very last mission. Mother of Mick flowers.

With machine-like efficiency I carefully flick a knife down the lower part of every stem, removing any thorns and foliage. Tedious as it is, correct prep is essential for the flowers to have a long and happy life.

When I worked in London - and I'm sure we'll get to it, but we don't have time for that long but not uninteresting story now - a German guy called Felix who was seriously OCD about correct prep trained me, and having that in my Skill Set has been a game changer.

I begin composing my bunch, starting with the glossy, dark camellia leaves as a base. Thankfully it all comes together beautifully. Every bloom fills its gap perfectly, every stem bending exactly the right way.

Holding it in my left hand, I cut off some twine and quickly but carefully tie it off using my right hand and my teeth. Mad skills, right...?

Carefully I trim every stem to the same length, then wrap them in wet cotton wool to keep them happy for the long drive home. Just as I'm tying a cellophane bag over the cotton wool, Ruby appears. Flustered and with slightly dilated pupils.

"Hot guy! In shop! For you!!!"

Once again, the entire workroom freezes and does their collective meerkat impersonation.

"No - he's here for *this* -" ...holding up my beautiful bunch... "And I don't know about *hot*...?"

"Oooh! *Hot!!!*" Ruby is nodding so emphatically her gleaming fire engine red bob ripples like silk. "And if you don't want him, here's my number..."

"Y'all gotta get out more..." shaking my head at her, I make my way out to the shop.

Action Man stands there, looking uncomfortable like most men do in a flower shop. He's wearing jeans and a military-style navy rib sweater with fabric epaulettes and elbow patches. I don't have to turn around to know there are twenty-plus people creeping up to the partition, trying to sneak a peek of him reflected in the many shop mirrors.

Upon seeing me, he looks suddenly relieved.

Then he notices the flowers, and looks completely awe-struck.

"Oh my God! They are incredible! Did you really do that???"

"Yup. One of my superpowers..." I reply, drily, as I wipe down the huge, dark marble shop counter and start laying out dark green paper to wrap them. I have a little attack of conscience, realising I've been a bit ungracious. "And thank you. I'm glad you're happy and I

108

hope your Mum likes them. I tried to remember everything Gran had told me about her... I thought pretty, feminine but strong, and a little bit wild would be the way to go..."

He nods, and for a split-second is almost emotional.

"Yep. That's her exactly."

I snip a length of luxurious periwinkle-blue taffeta ribbon and tie a perfect, fat bow. Mick hovers his watch over the EFT reader.

Right. Now for the tricky bit...

I've been very happy for the crazy-busy distraction all day, and it's been so nice *not* having to think about it, but I'm sorry to say the time has come...

I look up at him, frowning slightly.

"What...?"

"What... if I said there's a hit on Bo Marchesi tonight...?"

"And you know this how...?"

"Dream. Last night."

I pause, as everyone on the pretence of helping pack up the shop, is hovering, trying to eavesdrop and shamelessly checking Mick out whilst taking a ridiculously long time to pick up a vase of flowers.

"Are you finished for the day? C'mon, I'll drive you home and you can tell me on the way... And before you say no, it's raining, so you really don't want to walk..."

Ignoring a million questions from my pathologically nosey co-workers, I duck out to the workroom, grab my coat and handbag, and without making eye contact yell "Bye!" as I hustle out the front door.

I climb into the big white monster-truck. My body collapses in to the seat and I'm secretly very thankful I'm not having to walk. As I click in my seatbelt and we pull into the busy Saturday afternoon traffic, a wave of panic ripples from my heart to my toes.

"This is going to happen! *Tonight!* You need to *do* something!!!"

"What would you like me to do? Put Bo Marchesi under surveillance...? Place her in protective custody...? I can't just *do.* I need facts. I need evidence."

And once again... zero to borderline hysterical in three seconds. Just like old times...

"Seb Marchesi paid a hitman last night. He confirmed Bo's car. He confirmed tonight. What more do you want??? The hitman to drop you a fucking pin...???"

Abruptly he pulls over and turns to give me his undivided attention.

"Calm the fuck down! This is not helpful."

I inhale very slowly through my nose because I am possibly
about to explode with foreboding and frustration. Then he takes me
completely by surprise, reaching over and very carefully resting one
of his hands on mine.

Warm, strong and... strangely comforting.

"I believe you. You *know* I believe you. But you know you have
to give me something concrete... *anything*..." Blue eyes every colour
of the ocean are searching mine. Looking for clues. "Tell me what
you saw - but *only* what you saw... don't fill the gaps with what you
know... don't assume anything... Every single detail, any little thing
you can remember... C'mon, you can do it..."

And I do. The black leather gloves, the Aston, the voice, the
Range Rover... fast forward to the figure with Larry's body... deliberately neglecting to mention the love scene with Holly and my Karmageddon soft-porn debut...

We've arrived at the front of my building. He's frowning.

"So you didn't actually see or hear Sebastian Marchesi...?
You're only assuming that's him?"

"Who the fuck else would it be???" I'm a bit shrieky and more than a little hysterical. He's only got a few hours to save Bo... less Fact Man and more Action Man would be helpful.

"Anyone who owns black leather gloves and dislikes Bo Marchesi...? Doesn't narrow it down..."

"The Aston steering wheel...?"

"What? There's only one Aston Martin in Melbourne...?"

"Why are you being so fucking obstructionist???"

"Why are you being so emotional and illogical?"

"Because if anything happens to her, *it's all my fault!* And the fucking irony is... yesterday *I* could have cheerfully killed her, but... y'know... bitch lives *do* matter..."

He tries not to chuckle, but he can't help himself.

"Bitch lives matter..." shaking his head, he gently taps a finger on my temple. "What the hell goes on in there...???"

"Best not to know really... I wish I didn't have to a lot of the time..."

"Everything will be okay. Now get out - I gotta get back to work. I'll start with Aston SUV registrations... see what that turns up..."

I smile grimly and nod, getting out of the car.

Yes. At least that's a start...

"Don't put the heater on-"

"In the back seat... the flowers won't like it. Yes. You already said that..."

Saturday 4.25pm
What would Goldilocks do...???

I begin the trek up the many... many... stairs to my front door. Every kind of exhausted.

Too few hours of sleep...

Poor quality sleep due to psychic-induced nightmares....

Twelve hours of flat-out maximum output at work...

Stress/anxiety/distress from suppressing psychic-induced nightmares...

And the frustration that is Michael O'Malley in any circumstance other than a pool game...

Physically, emotionally and psychologically, this girl is cooked.

Simon is sitting on the sofa, flicking through a coffee table book about the Mitford sisters. He looks up at me, his cornflower blue eyes widened in alarm.

"Can I get you something? Cocktail...? Face mask...? Recreational drugs...?"

I shake my head.

"Sleep. I just need sleep. Like... ten beautiful hours..."

Simon leaps up and heads to my bedroom door.

"About that..." he murmurs evasively, blocking the doorway.

"What?"

"Somebody's been sleeping in your bed. And she's still there..."

"*What???*"

What the fuck is he talking about?

"Larry had such a bad day - I felt so sorry for her! She said she couldn't go home and face TBJ, so I suggested she take a nap... errr... in your bed..."

"*Larry had a bad day???*" I snarl incredulously. "She rocked up *five hours* late, couldn't find anything in her job description that appealed to her, and left five minutes later... How the fuck did she have a bad day...?"

Simon holds up his hands.

"Don't shoot the messenger! Do you want to sleep in my bed?"

"*No!* I want *my* bed! Fuck her!"

And with that, I storm into my room, kick off my boots and collapse onto my bed as violently as possible in the hope of waking her up.

However, I don't notice whether my plan is a success, because the second my head hits my pillow...

I'm out... for... the... count...

The grand proportions of the almost-black antique carved door swing open and Seb Marchesi walks in... Brown paper bags from various providores in one hand, gift wrapped bunch of hot pink and white variegated tulips in the other.

Oh fuck! The tulips...

It's real! All this is real...

Holly is sitting with her feet up on the sofa, a MacBook balanced in her lap. Bare feet, yoga pants and a cold-shoulder sweatshirt. No make up, black librarian glasses and her hair twisted hastily up out of the way in a clip...

She is beautiful.

Quietly coming up behind her, he bends down and gently kisses her bare shoulder. She tries not to smile, but can't help it.

"Just give me five minutes... I'm nearly finished..." her perfect brows furrow as she frowns at the screen.

He shakes his head, bemused.

"You don't have to do that..."

"And you don't have to cook..."

"I *like* cooking! I'm not allowed to at home - Sveta

yells something about peeling my turnip if I set foot in her kitchen…"

"And maybe I *like* doing books… so…" her eyes still focussed on the screen…. "What's for dinner…?"

"My nonna's Roast Chook! We blitz the skin to make it crispy, then cook it slow… It will be…*perfection!*"

He disappears into the kitchen, and after a little uncharacteristic banging and clattering, he returns with two glasses of pinot.

He deposits another kiss on her neck.

"I'm so sorry about last night…"

"It's okay," reaching back to run her fingers through his dark, curly hair. "It's not the worst thing you've done to me…"

"That's hardly a recommendation…"

"Mmmmm… Sebastian Marchesi. One Star. Would Not Recommend."

She tries to keep a straight face, but she starts giggling.

"Oh really?!" feigning offence, places the glasses on the coffee table. "How do I go about improving my rating…?"

"You could let me finish my quarterly tax statement…"

"Seriously - we can pay people to do that. You don't have to…"

"I *like* doing it! Entre Nous is my baby - I built it from nothing and I like to know what's happening... It's important to me..."

Entre Nous - her beauty salon. I know this because I'm her client. This whole thing - seeing them like this - creepy voyeur much...???

He raises an eyebrow at her, then sinks to his knees at her feet.

"I think I know how to get Five Stars..."

He starts softly kissing her toes.

Holly pauses, inhaling sharply.

Then his lips caress her big toe... and suddenly he sucks. Hard.

Eeeewwwww!!!

Hang on... Oh God! That is ridiculously good...!

Holly throws her head back and moans.

He proceeds to give every one of her nine other toes the same attention.

Each one has a slightly different intensity, but the general effect is the same. Apparently toe sucking is a crazy-erotic thing. Who knew...???

Not entirely carefully she places the laptop on the ground and collapses back on the sofa, luxuriating in his undivided attention.

His hands reach up and start pulling down her yoga pants...

Oh God! We're doing this? Seriously...?!

He yanks his chunky, charcoal designer sweater over his head.

Hmmm... he's in pretty good shape for mid-to-late fifties...

And then...

Oh good God no! I'm never going to be able to unsee this...

Unzips his designer jeans and suddenly he's completely naked and prowling over her half-naked body up to her lips.

He kisses her. Slowly. Passionately.

Damn he's a good kisser!

A confident hand slides up under her sweatshirt to find a perky little breast... as his equipment starts rubbing against...

Oh God! This is every kind of weird and wrong...

But...it's... good...

Holly gasps..

Ahhh! She's not the only one gasping...

With an agile little wriggle, her knees are bent and her smooth heels are resting on his buttocks.

Oh!... Well-played Holly!

Weird and wrong...? Yes, I'm aware of this but there's not much I can do about it, is there...?

Their gasps and moans get louder... more frequent... less con-trolled.

Heart rates increase as things steadily... rapidly... escalate.

Close... so close...

Holly cries out. Loudly.

Aftershocks of pleasure ripple right down to my toes.

She goes perfectly still. Breathing hard.

Seb collapses on top of her. Melted.

And is about to nuzzle her neck, when he stiffens a little...

"Do you smell smoke...?"

And right on cue, the ear-splitting bleating of the smoke alarm starts.

"Oh fuck! The chicken!"

He leaps to his feet and runs naked into the kitchen, which is filled with smoke. There's so much smoke I can't even see where the oven is...

And then it engulfs Seb, and he vanishes from sight.

All I can see is the smoke.

And hear the ear-splitting bleating of a high-pitched note re-peating over... and over...and over...

And then the smoke starts smelling like weird synthetic straw-berries and the ear-splitting monotone transitions to screeching feedback and is coming from all around me...

The dark room is crowded... and familiar. A couple of hundred people packed shoulder-to-shoulder.

Ewww! My shoes are sticking to the carpet.

Familiar. Very familiar.

The Thirsty Dog! My local pub at uni... the back room, where bands play live...

I'm way down the back, just in front of the bar. My right hand is holding two bottles of beer. In my left is a martini glass filled with red liquid that I somehow know is a Cosmopolitan.

What a bloody stupid choice of adult beverage! How the fuck do you not spill it...?

Three drinks. So I'm looking for two other people...

Who the hell orders a cocktail in the back bar of the Thirsty Dog...???

Simon! You're looking for Simon!!!

"Hey!" A friendly voice is in your ear as a hand gently grabs your forearm. The one holding the beers.

You turn to see a tall, skinny guy in a black hoodie. Emaciated, acne-scarred face. Pupils like pins. Outline of a teardrop tattooed under his eye.

A jolt of something uncomfortable but familiar.

Something is about to go very, very wrong...

He tries to smile. Thin lips and terrible teeth can only produce a skeletal grimace.

"Sorry mate! I thought you were Chelsea..."

I nod and try to smile.

Let's hope I don't look as disturbed as a I feel...

Through the haze, figures appear on the stage and the crowd surges forward.

A sudden explosion of noise - applause, cheering, whistling.

The screeching feedback becomes two notes.

Then a phrase.

Then drums and bass kick in.

Then a deep, commanding voice.

"Good evening and welcome to the QED experiment!"

Suddenly through the crowd, right down the front, there's a flash of yellow-blond hair.

Fluffy and sticking up like a baby chicken.

Simon!

I start wiggling my way through the tightly packed bodies.

Then the tall, skinny black hoodie reappears ahead of me... and I feel the most terrible sense of foreboding.

But it suddenly makes sense! It makes sense!

He was there last night... in my dream... at Karmageddon.

So it feels very, badly wrong but - hey! - at least it makes sense...

And he is also making a bee-line for Simon.

Why is this so bad...?

Then for a split-second the crowd parts and I see someone standing next to Simon...

Larry.

He's going for Larry!

I try to scream her name, but nothing comes out of my mouth. I need to get to her first, but my legs won't move fast enough.

A warm, sweet swelling noise.

Pure emotion - it sounds like the human heart.

Cello! No... it couldn't be...

Finally I get myself around a mountain of a guy in a red lumber-jack shirt and the whole stage is in view.

124

And there she is...

The lead singer is tall and dark. His overly-strong features are so distinctive it's hard to work out if he's handsome or just odd-looking.

"And bringing some class to proceedings, please give it up for the ravishing Sabine Goldblatt!"

Sabine!

My beautiful bestie since Grade 3. A very talented cellist, who after a chance encounter outside a recording studio swapped schlepping in an orchestra for minimum wage to being a session musician (and glamorous live gun-for-hire) in the rock industry.

What the hell is she doing playing Melbourne???

But Hoodie Guy is nearly at Simon and Larry...

And I can't seem to move fast enough...

A fist is crushing my heart... I can't breathe... I'm trying to yell... trying to scream but no words come out...

Sabine is closer. Sabine is right in front of her.

"Sabine!"

She can't hear me. She needs to hear me...

Screaming. In the dark. Over the almost deafening noise from the stack of Marshall speakers.

Screaming with everything I have...

"Sabine!"

She's laughing at something the lead singer said, her ash blonde hair twisted up in chopsticks. Looking so cool and sexy in black men's tuxedo pants and matching waistcoat - with nothing underneath but a glimpse of plum lace bra.

I'm screaming so hard it hurts... panicking... frustrated... choking back tears...

"Sabine! Get Larry! You have to get Larry!"

And suddenly Sabine is right next to me.

"Sid! It's okay! Larry is here. It's okay!"

No. No it's not okay. We could not be any further from fucking okay.

She's holding my arm. I shake her off, trying to break away from her.

I have to save Larry. Why will nobody fucking help me?"

"Sid!... Sid!... *Cressida!!!*"

She keeps shaking me and yelling my name.

She won't stop. She won't let go.

She keeps shaking me and yelling my name.

"Cressida!"

"CRESSIDA!!!"

Which is weird...

Because she never calls me Cressida...

You say dreams come true like it's a good thing...

It's like being underwater.

The yelling is distant.

Muffled and fuzzy.

Then it gets clearer.

Louder.

Closer.

"Cressida!!! Wake up!!!"

Sabine's voice. Uncharacteristically rattled.

Panic-stricken.

Vaguely it registers that the fingers digging uncomfortably into my forearms, shaking me, must be hers...

"What's she taken...? Look in the bedside table..."

"Nope. Nothing. She doesn't...-"

Larry's voice trails off. Small and scared.

"It's okay. She'll come to in a minute... She's started having nightmares. We're choosing to find it intriguing..."

Simon's voice. Trying to sound flippant but not entirely succeeding.

Tempting as it is to stay floating in the soft, fuzzy unconscious world, it is sadly time to go back...

Like being hauled up from a very long way underwater, I let the panicking voices and urgent hands pull me back to reality.

My eyes slowly open.

Sabine's dark, dark brown eyes are so close I can see noradrenaline has so dilated her pupils, they are almost black.

"Hi!" I whisper hoarsely. My throat feels red-raw. Hmmmm... Guessing I wasn't just screaming in my dream...

"Oh thank God! What the fuck...???" Sabine's fingers sink into my cheeks, desperately trying to hold me in the present.

Flat on my back, I stare vaguely at the ceiling.

Low-level queasy from my stomach to the back of my throat, like when you don't get to sleep off a hangover.

Larry and Simon appear in view.

Larry wide-eyed and alarmed.

Simon trying to be cool and blasé.

"Ah! There you are! Good of you to join us..."

Larry is frowning, looking most perturbed.

"You were screaming our names... like a mad woman! Where the hell were you??? And how did you know Sabine was here? That's... *trippy*..."

And all I can think of is one *very important* thing.

It is, actually, the only thing that matters right now.

A question.

And the answer is everything.

"What are you doing in Melbourne...?"

My green eyes search Sabine's so intently I can almost see her heart.

"Surprise gig... tonight. At the..."

And my heart starts plummeting, because I know what the next two words out of her mouth are going to be...

Thirsty Dog.

I take a long shower to wash some psychic angst down the drain and try to unpack what just happened.

So to summarise... drug-fucked loser in a black hoodie potentially poses a serious threat to Larry... and I just had virtual sex with Seb Marchesi.

Unsure which is more disturbing...

Mmmmm! The living room is toasty warm after the 'brisk' bathroom. Everyone - including the recent arrival of Danh - has congregated on our gigantic dark blue velvet couch. Still in my dressing gown (black silk kimono with red and gold dragons embroidered on the back) I grab a piece of capricciosa pizza from the box on the coffee table and perch on the curvaceous arm next to Sabine to eat it.

"You're a rubbish Jew..." I laugh at Sabine, as she stuffs one of the very non-Kosher pieces into her mouth.

"And you're a rubbish friend! I text my so-called Bestie when my plane touched down at *seven!* this morning and I'm *still* waiting for a reply! I had to knock on your door... with my Very Valuable hands!!!"

"Sorry Babe... You picked my second worst day of the year... It's so good to see you..." I give my favourite small, loud blonde girl in the world a big, squeezy hug, even though - actually specifically because - I can feel her cringe. She's not very touchy-feely.

"If I say I love you back will you let me go..."

Simon appears from the kitchen with a pitcher of cocktails.

Sabine holds up a hand to stop him.

"Count me out - I'm working tonight and it's going to need all the help it can get..."

"Really...?" Simon takes the rejection of his cocktails quite personally.

I glance around our living room.

"Where's Lucrezia...?"

"I put her in the kitchen. Thought it might be a bit warm in here for her..." Simon seems very proud of himself.

"Who the fuck is Lucrezia?" Danh looks bewildered.

"Lucrezia Borgia. My 'cello. Changes in temperature aren't great for her sound box and strings... She's temperamental... even by 'cello standards..."

"Temperamental by *cellist* standards..." I point a finger at Sabine.

In an elegant gesture, she flips the bird at me. Then her gaze returns to the cocktail jug.

"You know what? Hit me with one of them... It's going to be a clusterfuck tonight..." Sabine's long, ash blonde hair catches the light as she slowly shakes her head. "Fifteen egos, a random playlist, and after several hours of fucking around *forty minutes of actual rehearsal*... What could possibly go wrong...?"

"Who's playing...? Anyone I know...?" Simon's ability to capture personal style and instantly make people feel comfortable means he's worked with everyone from rockstars to royalty.

Sabine is so frustrated she actually snorts.

"*Everybody!* Quentin Darcy had the *genuis* idea to get all his famous friends together to perform a secret gig ... a supergroup called-"

"QED."

The letters come involuntarily right out of my mouth - and any chance that it could have possibly been just a bad dream flies right out the window. My nerves - which had only just calmed the fuck down - start jangling again.

And then I realise everyone is staring at me.

"How... could... you... *possibly*... know that???" Sabine is looking up at me like I'm a witch. "He's flown people in from everywhere - it's top secret... I only got in from New York this morning... He's announcing it live one hour before the gig... How could you know that???"

My eyes close and I take a deep breath. Because this is when it gets weird... and awkward... and uncomfortable... and scary.

So far, only a few people know about my new 'talent'... Simon, Mick, Gran... I guess I'd wanted to work out how to deal with it myself before I had to try explaining it to everyone. So I shrug vaguely and give the only logical answer...

"Oh... I dunno... lucky guess...?"

Simon, without saying a word, makes it very clear with one look from his cornflower blue eyes that he knows there are things I'm not telling. So before Simon or anyone else can start asking inconvenient questions, I change the subject.

"So... what were you doing in New York? Jealous much! Your life is sooo cool..."

"Y'all know Joe Falcon, right...?"

"*Omg!* Is he still alive...?" Danh is incredulous.

"Yep. Alive and well enough to try chasing girls around a recording studio..." Sabine rolls her eyes. She may be small and blonde, but she can look after herself. "Where he's remixing some stuff from decades ago. He needed some cello-ey shit to add some depth... someone gave him my number..."

"Hey - didn't he date the Boa... when she was working in New York...?" Simon... remembers everything. Misses nothing.

"Oooh yeah!" Sabine nods her head and laughs. "And he's *still* bitter... You can't say *Melbourne* without him hyperventilating..."

He also never misses an opportunity, and can't pass up even ancient history goss when it's straight from the source. He asks strategic questions and very quickly Sabine fills in the whole picture.

Bo, from very humble hometown Melbourne working class beginnings, worked/clawed her way to Supermodel Status. He was a rockstar. They were New York's number one Celebrity Couple. Then she decided she wanted more credibility and more power. She wanted to be top of the society food chain. So she dumped him and got herself noticed by the eldest son of politically aspirational Serious Old Money. And they dated for years, but no matter how hard she worked it, he would not propose. Apparently his mother couldn't stand her. And Bo was so fixated on making her dream of becoming First Lady manifest, she completely forgot about her US Visa. Immigration received an anonymous tip off about somebody outstaying their visa welcome... and a few hours later she was being unceremoniously bundled into a car, escorted through JFK and put onto an economy flight home... like a criminal.

"So she was... *thrown out of the country!!!*" Danh is beside himself with glee.

"Unable to ever enter the United States of America ever again, after being deported..."

"And not getting any younger, starts looking for the biggest fish in our little pond...?" Simon raises an eyebrow as he fills the gaps.

"Bingo!" sings Sabine. "Poor unsuspecting Sebastian Marchesi needed to stop playing the field and settle down... she was beautiful, famous, desirable... and apparently capable of keeping the *psycho* bit hidden until it was too late..."

I don't think anyone's ever described Seb Marchesi as 'poor and unsuspecting'... but anyway...

"And she never came to terms with having to settle for just owning Melbourne when she could have owned the world... which is why she's such a miserable c-" Danh seems to be enjoying this story a little too much.

"*Shit!*" Sabine has just noticed the time on the mantelpiece clock, "I gotta move! Can I grab a shower and steal some clothes?"

I'm just about to answer when Simon assumes control of the situation - and I'm more than happy to let him.

"Clean towels in the bathroom..." as he gestures to the door like a flight attendant pointing out the nearest exit... "What size are you? An Aussie eight??? How do you feel about a long Stevie Nicks kind of skirt? Or would you prefer pants...?"

"Yes to eight, yes to pants... no sleeves, please. It'll be hotter than hell in there - oh! Who's coming? I'll put your names on the door..."

I raise my hand.

"Like you have a choice, bitch..." she laughs at me. "Any more takers...?"

"Oh *me!*" Simon very enthusiastically raises his hand as he disappears into his office.

"You're not serious...!" Danh looks horrified. "The Thirsty Dog??? Brand new Gucci trainers on that sticky carpet...? Not happening."

"Don't you want to see what's happening on the street?" Simon takes his style watching very seriously.

"Not on that street, honey! I always feel like I'm about to be mugged..."

"ME!" Lovely Larry shoots her hand up, potential proximity to rockstars proving very motivating.

"*No!*" I almost yell at her.

Everyone turns to stare at me. Bewildered.

"Over-reaction much...?" Larry raises her eyebrows at me.

Yes. Very much. Too quick, too loud and too vehement.

Irrational even...

If you hadn't just seen the future...

So I have to come clean.

I tell them about the kidnapped girl on the boat. How I saved her life. Then I give them the second act of my dream - the Thirsty Dog scene, as accurately and with as much detail as I can recall.

They all end up looking equal parts disturbed, alarmed and skeptical.

"Why do *you* get to be psychic?" asks a very petulant Larry. "That's *so* unfair!"

"Will trade for your pathological sense of diminished responsibility... because that seems a whole lot more like fun. Trust me!" I reply sweetly.

But Simon, being Simon, is doing what he does... finding creative fashion solutions.

"So... if we don't see the guy in the red check shirt, it should be okay...?"

Hmmmm... I hadn't thought about it that way...

"Ye-eesss..." I agree, albeit *very* slowly - honestly I don't feel I've had enough psychic detective experience to say it with conviction. "I guess so... if we all stick together and watch our backs... it should be okay..."

Shouldn't it...?

A couple of hours later and we're in an Uber heading to the gig. Sabine and Lucrezia left earlier, and can I just say when Sabine emerged from Simon's office wearing black tuxedo pants and matching waistcoat, with a purple lace bra barely visible and her hair twisted into a sexy updo, which Danh had expertly secured with chopsticks, alarm bells started going off.

Last time - with the girl on the boat - I dreamt it as it happened. Like I was there. And there's been a handful of other little Real Time snippets... and a couple of retrospectives... But never the Future. Predictive Dreams are a whole new ball game - if it *is* actually predictive at all. However the more things I get 'right', the more seriously we should be taking this...

Right...???

It should be a very short ride to the Thirsty Dog. From our front door you follow the beautiful, tree-lined river bank for a few blocks. Look back at the picturesque city skyline with it's drizzling, winter mood-lighting and say *Ahhhh!*... Cross the river and head north, skirting the beautiful parks around the Melbourne Cricket Ground... then head into the formerly industrial, high-density urban maze that is the City of Melbourne's first suburb... Fitzroy.

"The tunnel's closed. You know why that is...?" Peter our angsty, middle-aged white man Uber driver asks rhetorically.

That a river runs through the middle of our pretty city is a traffic management nightmare. Options to cross it are limited - just one tunnel going each way and a handful of bridges. Each one is major arterial. And taking any one of them out of the equation results in an ETA disaster.

Larry's eyes light up. I give her a sisterly punch in the leg which says very clearly Do Not Engage.

But Lovely Larry cannot help herself...

"No! No, I do not. Perhaps you could tell us?" Larry is delighted to play ball. This is her favourite Uber driver - Conspiracy Pete.

"It's the children. They have to move the children!"

"What... children...?" Simon asks very slowly as he looks up from his phone, which forces me to give him a Do Not Engage punch too.

"The stolen children!" Pete's angst escalates to agitation. "The ones the government takes and keeps in the tunnels... they have to move them because of-"

"What, Pete? *What?!*" Larry is enjoying this far too much.

"The rain," Pete replies solemnly.

"Acid rain...?" asks Simon.

"*No!*" Conspiracy Pete's getting frustrated. Which is possibly his Default Setting... "Rain! Just... normal precipitation! Subterranean structures flood when it rains - *obviously!*"

For the rest of the journey, he is silent. Apparently this was a Test and we failed. Eventually he pulls up out the front of a Victorian-era hotel on a very busy nightlife street.

The infamous pub and live music venue, The Thirsty Dog.

We slam the car doors in relief and send Pete off to his next unsuspecting victims.

"You *had* to poke the bear, didn't you...?" I hiss at Larry.

She just giggles. As we've already demonstrated with Ash Knight, she's not a Good Decision Maker...

Larry and I - after the Simon and Danh makeover treatment - have a little strut in our steps, knowing that we're looking the hottest version of our Indie Chic Selves. Artfully messy hair. Pale and Interesting faces. Underground-cool black on black ensembles.

The queue to get in is snaking down the street and round the corner. In the nicest possible way, I make my way to the front of it and wait to catch the eye of the very big guy on the door.

And... *Bingo!*

"Look what the cat dragged in!" he smiles.

Meet Jackson, the surprisingly baby-faced chief of security. Big muscles, big laugh, big heart (but don't tell anyone) but *do not fuck with him.* I've often seen him in action when things get ugly - usually on a full moon... He does Muay Thai for fun, and can bring down and hold anything.

Without trying to make his job any more difficult than it already is - what, with hundreds of increasingly frustrated fans trying to scam their way in - I gesture subtly to the clipboard in his hand and mouth *We're on the list!*

Two barely perceptible nods. One at me and one over his shoulder towards the door.

Larry looks at me in amazement- and with a whole new respect.

143

"This used to be my playground..." I whisper, as we slip past the increasingly long and disgruntled line, leaving the cold, rainy Melbourne night behind us.

Right! Welcome to the Thirsty Dog.

To your left is the long, long front bar, so heavily populated with bar flies and dozens of dudes waiting for their name to come up on the pool table, one could not swing a cat. Should one be that way inclined...

However, we're going straight ahead... through the wide arched doorway into the back bar and band room.

It's already packed and the atmosphere is electric with anticipation, with everybody fortunate enough to be in here (and not waiting out there...) super-excited and a little bit smug. The air is thick with the disturbingly familiar smell of synthetic strawberry fog.

I grab Simon and Larry by the arm, pulling them close.

"Right! Stick with me and stay where I can see you... and if anyone spots the big guy in the red check shirt, we're outta here. Gottit...???"

They nod, possibly just to humour me.

And then I consider the possibility that maybe it all *was* just a bad dream, and we could be just about to have the most amazing night ever.

I guess all we can do is play Spot The Difference... and hope this isn't the sudden death round...

"So who's drinking what?" I ask the question, hoping for anything but...

"Beer!" from a very emphatic Larry.

"Can they do a Cosmo here...?" Simon looks equally hopeful and doubtful.

Oh fuck!

Hoping for anything but that...

The first sign...

That's not a good start...

There are people waiting four-deep to be served, but my mission takes a fraction of the time expected, thanks to the lovely pink hair'n'pierced Miss Sunday behind the bar. We played some pool and shared some banter back in my Bar Fly Days.

I turn back to the over-crowded room to find I've lost Larry and Simon.

Uh-oh!

Alone and holding two beers and a martini glass.

The second sign.

I try to scan the wall of bodies surrounding me, which isn't easy when most of them are taller than you... and you're trying not to spill a fucking Cosmopolitan...

There's a hand on my arm.

Butterflies of dread start fluttering in my stomach.

That would be sign number three.

Before they can speak, I spin around, expecting to see Skeletal Black Hoodie... and find myself looking at the coolest, prettiest girl imaginable.

Delicate, elf-like features and short pixie-cropped hair. A glimpse of bright green vintage Grateful Dead t-shirt under a vintage satin baseball jacket. She's smiling.

It's one of Simon's fashion friends, Indigo.

A loud sigh of relief.

Difference number one! Excellent.

"Hey! Cressida! Good to see you! Did you guys do Bo's party last night...?"

I look at her blankly. Last night??? Oh God! That was only last night... It seems like a lifetime ago. I remember she's now Melbourne editor for Vogue. She would have been top of the guest list...

Yes. I nod. Yes, I did.

"It was sublime. I loved the American in Paris meets Emily in Paris vibe... and the total largesse juxtaposed with the chic simplicity of total white... It was *so* Bo!" she throws her hands in the air, pretty eyes wide with wonder and enthusiasm.

Fashion People for some reason talk in sound bites that make everything exciting and significant. You get used to it.

"And I found a vintage white Balenciaga dress in an op shop for twenty bucks! Can you believe it???"

Yes I can. I'm sure Indigo's fashion radar and lucky shopping juju verge on witch-like...

We try to chat, but as the crowd, anticipation and noise level keeps escalating, every second sentence becomes *Sorry, what was that...?*

A pack of very fashiony people descend on her, shrieking like a flock of flamingos. She mouths *Later!* to me, and lets them carry her away.

And I am back to trying to find Larry and Simon in this sea of bodies. Seriously, what part of *stay where I can see you* is unclear…?

Suddenly my heart lurches up into my throat as I feel a hand grab my forearm.

A voice says "Hey!"

Oh God! No!!!

But logic starts talking down the panic.

Because it's a female voice.

Actually, it's a *familiar* female voice.

I turn to see Sabine. Her eyes are so manic they're almost twitching, her lips are clamped shut and she's breathing very slowly through her nostrils… which are flaring like a pissed off dragon.

Before I can say anything, she prises a beer out of my fingers and starts chugging.

"Shouldn't you be doing… something… backstage…?" I ask.

She shakes her head.

"I had to get out. Too many egos in one *very small* room…"

She takes another long slug from the bottle, then resumes the head shaking.

"If that tone deaf bitch tells me one more time I'm sharp, I'm going to pull a fucking chopstick out of my hair and fucking stab her..."

"Extreme... perhaps..." I'm starting to wonder if I'm actually getting any beer back...

"She is like *an entire semi-tone flat!!!* An entire semi-tone!"

I've no idea who She is, but I do know Sabine prides herself on having perfect pitch.

Sabine takes one long, last gulp, then returns the half-empty bottle with a flourish.

"Much better. Thank you. Hey, how do you manage to look extra hot when you're exhausted...? Your eyes are all smudgy and sexy..."

No idea how I do it, but yes, after two crazy psychic dreams and a freaking marathon day at work, I'm barely functional.

"Wish me luck! I'll come find you after the gig..." and she disappears into the crowd.

With my heart feeling a little lighter that maybe it *was* just a bad dream (and a little pumped that I apparently am looking extra hot...) I resume my search for Simon and Larry... hoping to find them before someone ends up wearing this freaking Cosmo.

I resume scanning the packed, dark room trying to discern actual people in the vague outline of shapes.

It's going to be okay, because that was all just a bad dream... right...?

"Hey!"

A friendly voice in my ear.

A hand grabs my forearm.

My skin prickles with recognition.

My heart starts thudding in my chest, in my ears.

And in a split second I know it wasn't just a dream.

Something very bad is about to happen to Larry.

We are go!

I turn and I see him.

Tall. Skinny. Black hoodie.

Teardrop tattoo. Emaciated acne-scarred face. Constricted pupils.

He tries to smile. Thin lips. Terrible teeth. Skeletal grimace.

He says the words *Sorry mate! I thought you were Chelsea.*

I feel myself nod and smile hopefully convincingly.

The band walks out onto the stage and the crowd surges forward.

I know I need to keep him in my sight. I try to follow him but he vanishes. I look around desperately but from the back every second person in here looks like him.

Screeching feedback becomes two notes.

Deafeningly loud.

Over and over.

Then they become a phrase. Drums and bass join in.

And then a voice.

Deep, articulate and authoritative.

"Good evening and welcome to the QED experiment!"

The crowd screams... applauds... whistles... cat calls...

Whatever *it* is, it's about to happen.

Panic rises. Uncontrollably.

I can't see. I can't make myself heard.

I can't find them first!

I start feeling sick.

Through the crowd I see a flash of yellow-blond hair. Right down the front. Fluffy and sticking up like a baby chicken.

Simon!

I start making my way through the crush of bodies.

Right on cue, the skinny black hoodie appears ahead of me... also making a bee-line for Simon.

Right on cue the crowd parts and for a second I can see Larry standing next to him. Laughing at something he's said. Carefree and beautiful.

And in grave danger.

A warm, sweet swelling noise from the stage.

Sabine making Lucrezia Borgia sing just like the human heart.

I can't see her, because a huge guy in a red check shirt is in the way.

Omg! The red check shirt! How could Simon and Larry miss him? We could be safely leaving now... we *should* be leaving now!

Quentin Darcy addresses his adoring fans. Tall, dark and either odd-looking or handsome.

"And bringing some class to proceedings, please give it up for the ravishing Sabine Goldblatt!"

I wiggle my way around the wide lumberjack shirt and see Sabine with a cool Mona Lisa smile, raise her bow to the crowd in a chilled salute.

Simon and Larry should be just in front of her...

Yes! Got them!

152

But in between you and them is Skeletal Hoodie Guy… Hovering…

I start pushing through people. Aggressive almost verging on rude.

I lose sight of Hoodie Guy, but I think I get to Simon and Larry first.

Simon grabs the glass out of my hand and swallows it in one gulp.

"Good God! Where the fuck have you been…? Literally *dying* of thirst here…"

I gesture urgently, jerking a thumb over my shoulder.

"*RED CHECK SHIRT!!!* Did you not see that…? It's fucking big enough!"

Simon looks at me blankly.

"That's not check, that's plaid."

"*Whatever!* Disaster Plan is *Go!* Grab Larry and don't let her go. We're leaving *now!*"

Larry shakes her head and mouths *No way!*

"*YES!*" I scream, trying to make myself heard over the surging, crashing noise from the stage.

Sabine has noticed. Her right arm continues to glide effortlessly over the strings, but she's watching us intently.

Then she starts scanning the audience around us. I know she's looking for Hoodie Guy. She gives a barely perceptible shrug.

This means *I can't see him* - I know her so well!

I feel the beginning of something. It's not quite relief, but there's a hopeful glimpse of tables maybe turning.

Sabine, from her perfect vantage point, can be our lookout. Hoodie Guy can't get close to Larry without her seeing!

So in actual fact, she's probably safer here than trying to fight our way through the hoards to the exit and out onto the street.

I concede to Larry and Simon that we can stay, then try to get into the eclectic band playing messed up cover versions of totally random songs.

We're four or five numbers into the set. They begin their dark and disturbed treatment of *Baby One More Time.* Suddenly Simon clutches at my arm.

"Fuck! I feel... *wrong...*"

His body feels limp as it half-collapses on me.

Sabine frowns at me, concerned... then her eyes widen in horror.

154

"Behind you!" she hisses.

Trying to hold up Simon, I glance over my shoulder and come face to face with Hoodie Guy.

He's staring at Simon, looking confused.

Simon is now halfway to the ground, about to collapse.

"I've been fucking roofied!" he slurs.

"*Help!*" I yell up at Sabine. Frantic.

She leans forward and deftly grabs the mic that was trained on Lucrezia's gleaming spruce belly.

"*Hey!* We need security. We need an ambulance. *Here!*" she yells clearly but urgently, as she points down at us with her bow.

And what happens next is a blur.

Abruptly the music stops.

The house lights come up.

The crowd parts like the Red Sea, as Simon sinks to the ground. Barely conscious.

I try to break his fall.

Looking around desperately for help, I see Hoodie Guy mutter *Fuck!* as he vanishes into the sea of bodies.

Jackson appears and picks up Simon like a doll, carrying him out onto the street.

A blur of flashing lights and a whir of sirens.

I make Jackson promise to get Larry home safely as I jump into the back of the ambulance.

The short ride to St Francis' takes barely minutes.

Hard, bright shiny surfaces and the unmistakeable smell of hospital...

Explaining what happened over and over again, as they wheel Simon into the triage ward.

Lying that I'm his girlfriend so I can fill out his paperwork. *Yes!* You have permission do bloods to find out which drug...

Answering the policeman officer's questions. Give description of Hoodie Guy. Try to make him take me seriously. Try to make it clear that I think he distracted me while someone else spiked the Cosmo. Vaguely realising that there's at least two of them...

Following the gurney up to a ward. Watching them tuck Simon's pale and suddenly very small body into the inhospitable narrow white bed.

Sinking into the equally inhospitable vinyl armchair next to the bed.

Overwhelmed. Exhausted. Emotional.

He's going to be okay. He was drugged. GHB. Acts quickly. Metabolises quickly. Lucky we got him tested quickly. His stomach has been pumped. He's on iv fluids. He'll feel rough tomorrow, but he's going to be okay.

I send a quick message to Danh.

Instantly my phone buzzes.

"What the actual fuck???"

"Someone slipped GHB in his drink. He's going to be okay."

"That's why I don't do the Thirsty Dog, honey. It's so... unsavoury..."

And then he explains that he doesn't do hospitals either, but volunteers to pick us up when Simon's released.

Which is at least one thing I don't have to think about...

And thought processes are proving challenging.

My head... my heart... my body... all shattered.

I cannot deny that I had another psychic dream...

but the transmission was a bit blurry in a few places...

There are things I got wrong.

I should have been watching Simon not Larry...

How do I fix that??? Must talk to Gran...

Hey! But without that heads up, what might have happened to Simon...?

I shudder, remembering Skeletor's face...

So while my instincts were apparently partially wrong, at least everything turned out okay.

Simon is safe. Larry is safe.

It's all over.

Except it isn't, is it...?

As I curl up into a little ball and let my eyes close... just for a second... there's that vague, niggling sensation of having forgotten something quite important... but I'm too tired to work out what that might be...

And just as I'm drifting off... there it is.

Bo Marchesi

What about Bo...???

Sitting in a car. In the dark. The wind outside is strong and wild, blowing raindrops onto the windscreen. A frosty chill radiates from the windows.

Waiting. Calmly. Confidently.

With the patience of an apex predator.

At regular intervals, casually glancing at the clock in the well-appointed dashboard.

Waiting.

The clock ticks over.

12.38

The engine purrs into life. The headlights aren't as bright as they should be. It's barely possible to make out the road a short distance in front of us.

Two lanes divided with double white lines.

Slick and gleaming with the rain.

Bordered with the narrowest of rocky shoulders and a safety barrier.

A beach road...?

The driver cracks their knuckles before placing black leather gloved hands on the Range Rover steering wheel. Their foot touches the accelerator softly a few times, gently revving the engine. Rhythmically their gaze moves between the clock and the road.

Lying in wait...

A white Porsche Cayenne flies past.

Bo Marchesi's car!

Calmly but decisively a foot depresses the accelerator and the Range Rover pulls out onto the road. In pursuit.

The inside lane is hard up against a rock face. All that's visible beyond the outside lane is a narrow, rocky shoulder and the safety barrier.

Beyond is a dark abyss.

Strong winds feel like they're blowing in straight off the ocean. The road is winding and treacherous.

The Porsche is driving it fast, taking the turns confidently.

We sit behind it at a safe distance, mimicking every turn. Waiting.

Oh...no... This is not good...

A stretch of straight road appears.

The Porsche guns it, pulling rapidly away.

Our driver floors it, catching up in seconds.

Blinding high beam lights flick on.

The Porsche swerves momentarily.

Without indicating, the Range Rover pulls out and starts moving up on the outside of the Porsche, like it's going to overtake, but-

Oh Good God no!!!

It hangs back for a second, lining up it's front quarter with the Porsche's rear wheel arch and with one perfectly timed bump sends the Porsche flying up in the air, over the safety barrier and into the black abyss beyond.

Of all the hospitals in the world...

And... *bang!*

I'm jolted wide awake, gasping for air.

I fumble with my phone.

Please answer! Please answer! Please answer! Pl-

"Good morning. To what do I owe the pleasure?"

Oh thank God! Mick not only answers, he sounds wide awake.

"Bo's gone over a cliff! You have to do something!"

"What...? When?"

I fill him in as quickly and accurately as I can.

He asks like a million very specific questions about the road.

"Are you sure...?"

"Of course I'm fucking sure! I saw her white Porsche get bumped off a cliff!"

"I'm on my way down to Mum's - I can cut through to the Ocean Road... I think I know the only place it could be - God it's an ugly drop... I can be there in thirty..."

Then he pauses and takes a very deep breath.

"I'm about to call the cavalry... I'm talking every kind of flashing light and probably choppers... if you've got this wrong, I'm going to look like an absolute dick..."

Lucky for him I'm too worried about Bo (oh! the irony...) to take offence.

"Mick! *I swear it happened!!!* I saw it in real time - I saw the clock on the dashboard... You have to help her!"

"On it! I'll keep you posted..."

So for thirty minutes I stare anxiously at my phone, scrolling distractedly and watching the minutes tick over.

Finally Mick calls.

"You were right! The vehicle has been located! Somehow it got stuck in trees halfway down so maybe... maybe she's alive..."

"Oh thank God!" my body sinks into the chair with relief.

All Psychic Nightmare Puzzles now solved.

Hopefully body count Zero.

Yay me!!!

"The SES guys are winching the car up now... The guard dog going off it's tits isn't making their life easy-"

"*What???*"

"There's a Dobermann going nuts - glad I'm not the one opening the car door..."

"Oh fuck! It's not Bo in the car - *it's Seb!!!*"

What the hell is going on???

"Seriously?"

"Yup. That's Seb's dog. Bo hates him... Seb doesn't go anywhere without him."

I overhear Mick yelling instructions.

In his element.

Commanding and capable.

"So Rich Girl... any ideas how we get Seb out of the vehicle without the dog killing us...?"

Right. This should work but Action Man probably isn't going to like it.

"His name's Nero. Tell him he's a good boy and you're going to look after his Dad. Then find his teddy-"

"His *what???*"

"His teddy. He has a pink dragon called Gary."

"You're fucking joking, aren't you?"

"Nope. No I am not."

I sink back into the chair and close my eyes.

I really should try to get some sleep. But my mind is whirring...

Wonder... relief... validation...

And awe... that I did indeed just have a legit Real Time psychic episode... followed by an overwhelming surge of so many emotions as it hits home that I actually just made a difference...

Then somewhere within the warm and fuzzies, there's that niggling feeling again...

I frown as I suddenly realise what should have been so obvious...

That should have been the last piece of the jigsaw but...

None of this makes sense!

Vibrations from my phone... it's an amazed-sounding Mick.

"You were right! It was Sebastian Marchesi!"

"Yup. Apparently I am somehow a legit psychic detective. Who knew...?"

"He's bloody lucky! He's unconscious but his injuries don't appear to be critical. He's been air-lifted to hospital..."

"And Nero's okay...?"

"He seems fine. They should take him for a vet check- *Jesus Candy!* Stop looking at him like that! I know it's your car, but we had to give him a ride back."

166

"Oh! You've got Nero...?"

"... and Gary..."

And Candy apparently. Seriously, how can anyone not like Nero...?

"I'll drop him home, then I want to talk to Marchesi... then hopefully get to Mum's in time for lunch..."

I nod slowly, relieved my favourite mogul is possibly not a murderer, and that he and his chief of security will live to charm their way through another day. But...

"Hey..." I say very slowly.

"What...?"

"There's something wrong here.... He never drives Bo's car... What are we missing?"

"I know. It doesn't smell right - *Candy! I can see you giving him side eye! Knock it off! Please!*- A squad car went to the Marchesi house... could only speak to the housekeeper. Bo was doped up on sleeping pills - hey! I gotta take this call. Get some sleep, yeah...?"

Highly unlikely, Action Man.

Highly... unlikely...

So many things whirring around in my head...

Let's unpack it, shall we...?

We have Seb Marchesi run off a road he shouldn't have been on... in a car he shouldn't have been driving... last seen (ahem!) naked on the couch with his girlfriend this afternoon... then we have Simon getting roofied when I thought it was going to be Larry... Oh! the same Larry who is also having an affair with the very married Ash Knight... And poor Nero! He must be so confused and worried... and then there's the disturbing problem of how Mick's voice changed when he told me to get some sleep... It *did* go a bit... soft, right...? That was not my imagination... Candy! What a piece of work!... but nice guys always have bitch girlfriends, right...?... Not that I think Action Man is *nice*... no!... not at all... Anything else...? Oh God! It's Mother's Day... not that many hours til I have to be at Gran's for lunch... ah! Gran! I'll be able to have a chat to Gran... Oh shit! I have to deliver Bo's Mother's Day stuff too... and the flowers for Mick's mum... he needs to put them in water... it's too long... far too long without... water...

And sleep...

Far too long without sleep...

I curl up sideways in the chair and let my eyes close for a second. I yawn, resting my cheek on the vinyl.

Why are hospitals always that little bit too warm...?

It's proving quite difficult to open my eyes, so I'll keep them closed...

Just for... a ... second...

I'm standing in a long, long empty corridor.

It's Karmageddon, but it's not...

Doors at either end. And a portrait in the middle.

An apparently naked Bollywood cartoon version of me sitting on an apparently naked cartoon of Ash Knight.

What the...???

I'm freezing cold and my feet are killing me.

Larry appears, way down the other end. She's screaming into her phone... at Ash Knight.

A figure in a black hoodie appears behind her, picks her up and calmly carries her out the door.

I try to scream, but no words come out.

But it's up to me!

It's all up to me...

I try to run, but my legs can barely move.

There's nobody in sight.

Nobody else can save her.

It's all up to me...

I somehow stagger through a doorway and into the chaos of Karmageddon.

Packed with a loud crowd and even louder music.

Lavish, ornate and over-the-top... like a Bollywood version of an Indian palace.

Desperately I search for someone to help me, I beg every face for help.

But there are only strangers who ignore me.

Where does the door go...? frantically I ask everyone. But nobody answers me.

People are holding a champagne glasses... and Seb Marchesi is proposing a toast.

And now everyone is here...

Simon, Sabine, Danh...

Sveta… and Bo Marchesi, wearing a #bitchlivesmatter t-shirt.

Mick, tossing kofta balls at Nero… who is catching them with a confident *snap!*.

Rory, holding a drink in one hand for himself, and one in the other that he's waving at me…

"To Cressida! It's all up to her!" proclaims Seb joyously.

"It's all up to her!" the whole room replies enthusiastically. There's a *crash!* as Sveta flings her empty glass and it shatters into hundreds of tiny, sparkling pieces.

For a second, all I can think of is Nero cutting his feet. Someone really needs to clean up that glass…

It's all up to me.

It's all up to me.

I feel a tap on my shoulder.

I spin around to find myself face to face with Ash Knight.

"You were asking about the door…?" his voice is smooth and offhand. "It goes up to the roof… it goes up…"

"What goes up, must come down… Universal Law of Gravitation!" Sveta enthuses.

"Larry…?"

Something is about to happen to Larry.

Sveta looks at me like I have two heads.

"No. Sir Isaac Newton... What does she weigh? Gravitational acceleration 9.8 metres per second squared... would be easier if they had whiteboard in here..."

Suddenly fear gives way to dread, and everything goes from weird to badly wrong.

Seb Marchesi is pointing out the huge windows and laughing so hard he can barely get the words out.

"Shouldn't you be doing something about that...? Isn't it all up to you...?"

"They show her where lobsters spend the winter..." Sveta nods knowingly.

Larry's limp body appears fleetingly, falling in slow-motion through the air, before plummeting seven floors to the ground.

I wake up with a start. Disturbed and confused.

There's some seriously surreal shit going on there, right...? So while I'm pretty sure that's not psychic, I don't want to think about what a psychoanalyst would make of it...

Where the lobsters spend winter???

What the fuck does that even mean...?

9.8 metres per second squared???

There's obviously only one thing to do.

I perform a quick Google fact check, then stare at my phone in total amazement.

Where the hell did that come from?

I'm pretty sure I slept through every Physics class...

I sigh and give Simon a little poke. More out of boredom than concern... He doesn't react. Just keeps breathing almost unnaturally slowly and deeply.

Remembering I haven't eaten anything since the pizza too many hours ago, I slip out of the ward in search of a vending machine.

I prowl the dimly lit, deserted corridors, feeling like somebody should be stopping me and asking me what I'm up to...

But nobody does.

Having no success, I jump into the lift to extend my radius.

Up or down...?

Less traffic on higher floors should increase the chances of a better-stocked vending machine...?

Sounds like a plan.

I press number six. *Neurology.*

The gamble pays off! The doors open onto a little lobby with a vending machine. With one packet of Maltesers left.

I tap my card and punch in the code.

The shiny red packet of heavenly little chocolate and malt balls starts sliding towards me, but just as it's about to drop, it freezes. Stuck.

"Oh no no no no no!" I mutter. "Do not fuck with me..."

I bump the glass as hard as I can, slamming it with a solid hip'n'shoulder. The packet trembles for a second, then free-falls to the tray at the bottom.

"That had better not be the last packet of Maltesers, because I will fight you for them..." a familiar voice behind me threatens.

Part amused, part bored... with a strong overtone of exhaustion. Rich and resonant, sticky like treacle.

Slowly shaking my head, I turn around to see a familiar handsome face and (too!) familiar tallish, lean body looking unfamiliar in scrubs, with his shoulder-length auburn hair slicked back into a professional ponytail.

"Of all the vending machines on all the floors in all the world, she crashes into mine..."

Meet Dr Jamie Wolfe. One of the very handsome skeletons in my closet. Too late I remember that he's specialising in neurology... at this hospital...

"... and takes his last packet of Maltesers..." I laugh slyly, shaking the bag in front of him.

"Are you a figment of my over-tired imagination?"

"Oh no! I'm very real..." as I open the packet and pop one in my mouth, "... as are the Maltesers..."

"Remember when I ate Maltesers out of your belly button...?"

"Remember all those times you said you'd call, and you didn't...?" I reply sweetly, with a raised eyebrow, through a mouthful of chocolate. The skeleton of Dr Jamie was buried a very long time ago, so this is actually pretty funny. Enjoyable even.

"And now you're the one not calling me... I gave you my number like, a *month* ago..."

"I know, right...? No *emergencies*, I guess..."

"So why are you on my floor at 3am...?"

"Oh yeah... *actual* emergency... Simon got roofied. He's sleeping it off... I'm bored and hungry... which possibly could also constitute an emergency..."

"GHB? Shit. There's a lot of it on the street right now." He frowns at me, looking concerned. "Be careful!"

"You say that almost like you care..." I tease him.

He's frowning, possibly about to say something serious when there's a soft *ding!* and the elevator doors slide open, revealing a patient on a gurney surrounded by a small army of anxious people in scrubs.

Saved by the bell. Literally!

"Ah! This is what they dragged me out of bed for..." he sighs, then inhales slowly, kicking himself into Professional Mode.

Despite knowing that he would not have left an empty bed, I take pity on him and hand him the half-empty... or half-full!... little red packet.

"Baby Girl has a heart!" he laughs, taking it from my hand and upending it over his mouth.

I'm just about to retort with something sassy, when I hear a croaky voice calling my name.

There on the gurney, connected to an iv, is a pale, bruised and battered Sebastian Marchesi.

Jamie looks bewildered.

"You... know... him...?"

I rush to his side. The medical team get very prickly and defensive, but there are like a million questions I need to ask him. He beckons me to lean in close.

When my ear is almost at his lips, he whispers urgently but with considerable effort-

"My girls!"

Agitated and panic-stricken.

"They're stealing my girls!!!"

"Your girls are all fine," I say softly and hopefully reassuringly. "Is there anything you need to *tell them...*?"

Maybe if he can get a message to Holly, he'll calm down.

"No..." now he's the one looking at me like I'm crazy, as he mutters "... that's ridiculous... Tell Holly I'm okay and leave her a chicken..."

He's delirious, right…? *A chicken…???*

"Don't you mean flowers?" I ask gently.

"No!" he is quite adamant. "A chicken… A roast chicken… It's a joke…"

As his voice trails off, I finally get it.

The chicken that nearly set the penthouse on fire…

I start nodding knowingly, then remember that I'm not supposed to be knowing any of that. It's bloody hard work being psychic. Just sayin'…

His eyes widen in alarm.

"Nero! Where's Nero??? "

I reassure him that Nero is fine and Nero is safe.

He closes his eyes and seems to relax a little.

An uppity and hostile nurse who's been hovering the whole time sees the opportunity to get rid of me and seizes the moment.

"How are you even here? Who are you??? Mr Marchesi needs to rest… but first he needs to see the neurosurgeon!"

Everyone turns to look at Jamie, who holds up a finger to pause the attention while he scoffs the last surviving Maltesers.

"And that would be me..." as he begins scanning Seb's chart. "Hi Mr Marchesi - I'm Dr Jamie Wolfe. Seems every other department has had a crack at you tonight... and now it's my turn..."

Seb smiles weakly. I turn to go, but he grabs for my hand.

"Thank you..." he whispers hoarsely.

And I know I *should* go... but I really need to know...

"What were you doing on that road...? In Bo's car...?"

"The girls! The alarm... the cameras... loading my girls into a truck... Aston at Chou Chou... had to take the Cayenne..."

Before I can ask any more questions, he's whisked somewhat aggressively into a private room.

Hmmm...

Ain't no-one getting any sense out of him anytime soon...

I stare blankly at the lift doors... waiting... wondering what time they'll let me break Simon out of here.

Ding!

The doors slide open, and I'm face to face with Svetlana and the Marchesi kids. Max has his hands buried in his hoodie, trying to look stoic and be a Big Man... but he can't hide the fear in his eyes. Ava is not even pretending, both of her arms wrapped around Sveta, clutching her like a toddler. Looking little, scared and vulnerable in her unicorn-covered oodie. Svetlana's mouth is set grimly and her eyes are narrowed purposefully.

They all look confused to see me.

Oh yeah… I am very much out of context and looking considerably more glamorous than usual.

"I just spoke to him! He's doing okay."

They now look even more confused…

I tell the Simon story, then the Seb story as quickly and economically as possible. They look too overwhelmed and worried to be trying to process superfluous information.

"What about Nero…? Where's Nero??? Is he okay…?" Ava seems almost too scared to ask.

"He seems fine. He's with a friend of mine - Mick. He's a cop… he was at the scene… he's bringing him home now."

You can see the relief almost melt her.

"And Mr Marchesi is with the neurologist, Dr Wolfe… he's excellent… he's also friend of mine…"

"You gotta lotta friends…" Max observes, almost impressed.

"Melbourne. Small town…"

"You know doctor? You come with us."

Sveta grabs my arm and steers us all to the waiting area - uncomfortable chairs and a coffee table covered with magazines.

My eye instantly goes to the current issue of Vogue.

The cherry red masthead matches the model's cherry red ski suit, which is unzipped to the breast bone. Shot seemingly in a blizzard, she's wearing a glossy fur cossack hat and is laughing as she catches snowflakes on her tongue… her brilliant aquamarine eyes sparkling.

Ava surreptitiously reaches to turn the magazine face-down.

"You look amazing! Own that shit!"

"I was freezing… it was in Japan…" is Ava's quiet and embarrassed reply.

"Hat was my idea!" Sveta chimes in, proudly.

"Who even *are* you…? Who's the bougie babe??? Where's my little stinker…?" Max puts her in a head-lock. She pokes him hard right in the belly button. "Ow!!! Disturbing accuracy… disturbing… So the Big Dog sounded okay…?" he asks hopefully.

"Hmmm… maybe a little delirious. He kept saying someone was stealing his girls…"

"Da! Alarm went off. That's why he go." Sveta nods grimly.

What???

"His girls...?" My mind starts flicking through scenarios. None of them good. Strip Club. Exotic Dancers. Human Trafficking???!!! *Surely not...*

"*Cars!*" Max explains very slowly. Like I'm mentally deficient. "Like a hundred mint cars! Seriously *valid!*... oh and a few randoms... gives them girls' names because they give him a stiffy-"

Biff! Sveta slaps him in the back of the head.

"No speaking dirty around your baby sister!"

And suddenly it might start making sense.

It was a trap...???

"Was there a break in...? Has anyone checked?"

Max suddenly looks very interested in the conversation.

"Get coffee!" Sveta hands him her card and gestures to the vending machine.

"Nah. All good thanks."

"Get *me* coffee - get her one too... Da...? And hot chocolate for your sister..."

"Da-ya-ya-ya..." he mutters, dragging his feet.

When he's out of earshot, she murmurs -

"Alarms go off... a dozen men in the garage - you can see on the cameras... *Stealing!*... Ivan go... then when Ivan get there... *nothing!* All cars still there."

Omfg!

She looks me right in the eye, nodding slowly.

"Accident...? *Puh!* Someone show him where the lobsters spend-"

And we both say at exactly the same time....

"Winter."

My mind whirs and right down in my gut, faint unease gives way to a tidal wave of disquiet.

But... but... but...

So many questions...

I'm trying to work out where to begin when Jamie appears.

"You're Svetlana...? He's asking to see you. He has a broken collar bone, cracked ribs and severe concussion. We need to monitor that, so he'll be in for observation for a few days. He's a lucky man... That accident should have killed him..."

Sveta's eyes narrow almost imperceptibly at the word *accident.*

"I go see him now-" she doesn't ask for permission. It's a statement.

"Just a few minutes. He needs to rest…"

And Jamie ushers Sveta and the two Mini Marchesis into Sebastian's room. Much as I'm dying to ask more questions, I know it's not my place right now.

The lift doors slide open and I jump in.

As I turn back, I see Jamie hovering.

Waiting for me to look.

"Call me! he mouths silently at me, holding an empty hand to his ear.

With a little ironic snort, I shake my head and laugh quietly.

"Not a chance!" I silently mouth back as the doors slide shut and take me back to Simon.

One Mother of a Sunday...

It's more than a little chilly, but with fortunately clear blue skies as I'm walking to work a few hours later.

Simon eventually woke up like nothing had happened and Danh drove us home, with time for a couple of hours snooze. Which wasn't enough... felt like I'd only just got to sleep when the freaking alarm went off...

Ideally nobody's going to see me, so I'm dressed pretty low-key. Jeans, black cashmere turtleneck, puffer jacket and snow boots. Gloves would be good, but eating a piece of warm banana bread (dripping with butter!) is frankly more important than circulation to my fingers.

This is when I'm super-thankful for the little cafe, Right Side of the River, a couple of doors down from our building. TBJ would say eating whilst walking is a Bad Eating Behaviour, but I'd call knocking over coffee and brekky without having to stop Efficient Multitasking.

Two chunky-bodied ravens - their black feathers gleaming in the sunlight - are picking through the litter of autumn leaves under the big, naked trees.

Two for mirth...

A car horn honks. They look up with a start for a second, feathers ruffled, then resume their treasure hunt. I ignore it and keep walking. It's inner-city. Happens all the time.

The car honks again. Louder. More insistently.

This time they stop, and we all turn in unison to glare at the culprit.

A white Toyota HiLux. With a familiar face behind the wheel and a familiar black-and-tan dog (with a pink dragon) in the passenger seat.

"Get in!" he yells, winding down his window.

"Are you stalking me...?"

"*Get in!* I don't have time for this!"

Only because it'll save me a few minutes... and it's pretty cold... and I want to see Nero... and yes, Mum, it's better for my digestion... I open the passenger door and squeeze in next to Nero.

"Hey Handsome! How you doin'? You want some banana bread...?"

"No thanks, I'm- oh! You're talking to the dog..." He sounds a little disappointed. "Can you drop him home? No one answered when I tried last night... Seb Marchesi said you'd be doing a delivery this morning?"

"Of course. If he's okay with slumming it in a work van..."

He leans in, gently dropping Gary in my lap and resting his head on my shoulder.

I guess that's a Yes...

"So... whaddya know...???" I ask through a mouthful of food, because I have so many questions I don't know where to start. And I'm guessing that even though it's probably not Federal Cop jurisdiction, he'll have ways of finding shit out...

"The alarm went off at his beach house..." he begins as he pulls away from the curb. "He keeps his car collection there... he was going to investigate... he was accidentally pushed off the road by someone driving erratically-"

"But-"

"That's his story and he's sticking to it. The alarm must be faulty - there's nothing to suggest a break-in-"

"But there's security footage of cars being stolen..."

"And... how would you know that...?" he asks very slowly.

"Svetlana the housekeeper told me. I bumped into her at the hospital."

"What the fuck were you doing at the hospital? Do we need to have another chat about not interfering...?"

So... last time I was braver than I ever knew I could be, and did something I probably should not have...

Okay. So following a serial killer onto his SuperYacht and getting myself locked in his purpose-built dungeon is not the smartest thing I've ever done...

But, hey! Nobody died, right...?

"Calm down... I was there with Simon. He got roofied-"

"GHB? Is he okay...? There's a lot of it on the street right now..."

"He's fine. His liver's pretty match-fit when it comes to metabolising drugs-" *Oh shit!* I probably shouldn't say that to a Fed...

"Glad he's okay. And I didn't hear the second bit... So what *exactly* did the housekeeper tell you...?"

I fill him in. By which time we've almost arrived at Le Jardin. I direct him up the maze of bluestone laneways to the back door. There's no way I'm opening the front door on M-Day. I'd be mobbed!

I really need to get out of the car and get this stuff delivered to Casa Marchesi, but something's really bugging me.

"So… who knew he would leave his car at ChouChou and would have to drive Bo's car…?"

"Apparently he does it all the time when he goes to the footy. Drives to the club to do some work, leaves the car there, has some beers at the game and gets an Uber home… Pretty common knowledge. Anyone could know…"

"Ri-ight… the football…" So that's what he tells Bo when he wants to spend time with Holly… Pretty good cover. Buys him easily five hours and it doesn't interest Bo enough for her to ask difficult questions.

"What?" he pounces on me right away. He misses absolutely nothing. "What do you know…?"

I'm about to attempt to deflect, when I notice something on the back seat.

"Oh shit! The flowers!!!" I cry out, alarmed and more than a little horrified at how long my beautiful bunch has been sitting in his car out of water. "You bring Nero in, I'll get these…"

"It'll be fine-"

"No. They won't be! And it's my fault you didn't get to your Mum's last night… Please! Let me fix them. It won't take long…"

So with both boys not knowing quite what to do with themselves - Mick leaning awkwardly on the work bench, and Nero frozen in an equally awkward, perfectly neat sit - I get to work.

Grabbing a glass vase that won't be missed, I carefully re-trim the ends of all the stems and rearrange them in the cool, clean water.

"Oh! Isn't that better...?" I ask them.

Lucky it was so cold overnight. It's not a great thing to do to them, but at least it wasn't disastrous.

I sit the vase in a carton, and tightly pack big balls of rolled up paper around it to keep it steady.

Fleetingly, Action Man becomes a human being and gives me one of his too-rare smiles.

"Thank you! You didn't have to do that... It's beautiful! Mum will love it..."

And for a second, I think he's going to hug me.

Which passes.

I fish three bunches of chrysanthemums out of the cool room and start gift wrapping them. Generally not a fan of the common daisy-like chryssie, but these are insanely perfect, giant fluffy pom-poms - palest pink for TBJ, spectacular mauve for Gran and brilliant lime for my sister, Miranda, who's only been a Mama for about a month.

Grabbing the keys to my favourite work van, I eyeball the very impressive gardenia sitting on the bench, complete with Seb's envelope attached to a luxe moss green satin bow with a tasteful pearl pin. In a gorgeous Tuscan terracotta pot...

A very heavy looking terracotta pot...

"You are seriously not picking that up!"

Why does he constantly feel the need to try to tell me what to do???

"Oh but I am... *Very seriously...* Occupational hazard, Action Man..."

"Why are you so obstinate???"

"Oooh! Big word!" as I get ready to lift this sucker.

But before I can, he's reaching over and with a grunt lifts in onto his hip.

I hum a dramatic interpretation of Mariah's *Hero* as I direct him out to the van.

"Fuck off!" he mutters as he carefully places it just inside the sliding door.

"Seriously, you need to fuck off! Isn't it like three hours to your Mum's house..?"

"Yep. Yep, it is... Later, Rich Girl."

"Later, Action Man."

At Casa Marchesi, something isn't right.

Svetlana isn't there to greet me.

The front door is ajar.

Holding the precious little rose posy from Ava, I tentatively call out -

"Hello? Anyone home...? It's Cressida from Le Jardin..."

Nero, holding Gary in his mouth, looks up at me with a slight frown, then flicks the door open with his nose and walks bravely inside.

I follow him. It is, after all, his house.

He pauses outside Bo's study.

I can just hear her voice.

Low and hissing. *Very angry.*

"I don't care if you attempted it, the delivery was not received. I'm not paying any more until it's done. And I want it done tonight!"

Brief silence before she replies.

Coldly and quietly.

Seething.

"None of this is my problem! I need it done! Surely you have ways of delivering to the hospital..."

Another brief silence. Apparently she gets the right answer.

"Okay. Tomorrow night. I'll make sure he's still there-"

A pause while she's interrupted.

"More money? You fucked up! Why would I pay you more money??? Just get it done."

I'm frozen to the spot with my heart in my mouth and my pulse thudding in my ears.

In a blinding flash, it all becomes clear.

She was driving Seb's Aston.

She paid the hitman.

She knew Seb would be driving her car.

It's not a delivery. It's a dispatch.

A permanent one.

And just as all the dots are joining up in my head, the door swings open and I'm face to face with the Boa.

Before I can try to speak, she glares at Nero and starts shrieking.

"What the fuck is that doing here??? Get it out of here! Now!!! Take it to the pound for all I care..."

I inhale very slowly through my nose.

Initially it was to steady my nerves, but it's escalated to subduing my anger. Abhorrent enough that she's trying to kill her husband, but to be mean to his dog is possibly the last straw.

"Happy Mothers' Day!" I exclaim through gritted teeth, with a big, fake smile.

She just grunts, takes the posy from my hand without even looking at it and throws it onto the sideboard.

"Is that all?"

I can't work out if she means is there anything else or if she's complaining about the lack of extravagance.

"There's also something from Mr Marchesi..."

"Ugh!... Leave it on the front steps. And take his mutt with you when you go..."

Nimble as a cat, Nero jumps up into the passenger seat of the van and settles in to ride shotgun.

"Yep. I wouldn't want to stay with her either, Mate."

I sit for a second staring blankly at the divine - and unappreciated - Gardenia, lonely and abandoned on the grand front steps... my mind whirring.

What to do... what to do...

Taking a deep breath, I find Seb Marchesi in my Contacts.

Hey! The delivery that failed last night is rescheduled for tomorrow night.

At the hospital

Please let him have his phone!

And please let him understand what that means... and be vague enough in case somebody else who shouldn't reads it!

Seconds later I get a *Thumbs Up* emoji.

Followed by

Ivan's on it.

Thought that might be the case...

Call in early as poss tomo morning - have a job for you

I reply with a *Thumbs Up* and as I prepare to drive out, he surprises me with another message.

and Thank You!

for everything.

Hitting the road, I ask Siri to call Mick. Bah! It goes straight to voicemail...

Damndamndamn!

I leave a somewhat convoluted message, then exhale. Long and deep. Mother's Day is a big thing in my family... hopefully I've done everything I can to help everyone I'm supposed to for now, and I can just enjoy the rest of the day.

Hopefully...

"Anyone can be good in the country..." Oscar Wilde

The phone rings three times before a calm, quietly authoritative Scottish male voice picks up.

"Laurence Carlisle... to whom am I speaking?"

This is my grandfather, and the fact that he is indeed answering a land line phone will give you some idea how Old School he is...

"Hi Grandpa! Is it okay if I bring a few extras...?"

"Of course, dear! The more the merrier! Must dash - before my creme anglaise becomes scrambled eggs... See you soon dear-"

Click! He hangs up on me.

So... they are expecting me... and Simon, whose family are all in Perth, way over on the other side of the country. They are not expecting Danh, Sabine... and Nero.

We're all packed into Danh's sporty little black Mercedes. He's at the wheel (and driving in a frustratingly cautious manner that does nothing to disbunk racial stereotypes...)

I'm in the front passenger seat, trying not to fall asleep whilst navigating (and pumping an invisible accelerator...)

Simon and Sabine are in the backseat, both looking worse for wear but for very different reasons.

And Nero (with Gary, obviously) is perched neatly on the seat between them, sporting a black *Brooklyn* beanie, puffer vest, Aviators and an epic gold Chanel necklace.

"It's his Gangsta Look..." Simon explains, beside himself with enthusiasm that he has a new victim to play Dress Ups with. Nero poses like a pro while Simon takes pics.

"Do you have Ava's number...? I'll send her these for his Insta..."

The dog has his own account...? Well, *Duh*!

"Flick them to me and I'll forward it to Sveta - hopefully it'll cheer them all up a bit..."

"Hey Nero! Can we try a few without Gary...?"

Nero delicately drops his dragon in Sabine's lap, and pulls himself up to his full height, looking regally down his nose... while Sabine also looks down her nose, but in mild disgust at plush pink thing.

"Oh! That's fantastic! *Yes!*" Simon enthuses, clicking away.

"Did I mention I'm actually more of a Cat Person...?" Sabine protests half-heartedly before arranging her face into a cool pout and leaning into the shot with peace sign fingers.

Sabine spills the tea on what happened in her world last night. The gig resuming... on-stage Pitch War with the sexy-but-not-very-talented back-up singer... Lovely Larry very much loving having her own personal bodyguard, Jackson... Lovely Larry partying on with the band and very much enjoying Celebrity By Association status... Sabine dropping Larry home at 7am, then meeting her mother for breakfast... which did not go well... which is why she's in the car to spend the rest of M-Day with my family...

We negotiate the network of bridges, skirting the gleaming concrete and glass city on one side, and the vast dock yards heading to the perfectly still, grey bay on the other...

Then we hit the open freeway...

Freeway becomes highway... then highway becomes bumpy country road.

After driving for considerably longer than we should have, thanks to Danh's reluctance to move out of the slow lane, we finally arrive at my grandparents' farm. I spent a lot of time here growing up. It will always be one of my Happy Places.

Grandpa isn't technically a farmer. He's a lawyer - like most of my family. Despite the big retirement party a few years ago, he still goes into the office most days. He's kind of a big deal - he was asked to be a judge but he said no.

Because he's intelligent, patient, diligent and lucky, he seems to succeed at pretty much anything he tries.

This is more than partly due to his ability to attract talented, passionate people and trust them do their thing. With the help of a farm manager and a winemaker, dabbling in Angus Cattle became a lucrative stud farm... planting some grapes became an note-worthy vineyard... and then there's the horse he won in a bet, who became a Group 1 winning thoroughbred (and is now enjoying retirement as pet and lawnmower at the farm).

Eventually a long stretch of white post and rail fencing comes into view.

"So see the avenue of giant trees coming up...? There's a gate...you're turning right..." I direct Danh, who instantly slows to a crawl.

"Oh... where...? Here...? Here...? Are we there yet...?"

"*Here!*" as a big wrought iron gate with 'Verity Park' emblazoned across the middle appears. I hit an app on my phone and the gate starts swinging slowly open. They may be Old School, but ain't nobody wants to get out of the car to open these suckers in the rain...

With an indignant wiggle of his tail feathers, the raven who was sunning himself on the top rail spreads his wings and leads the way to the front door.

The journey from the road to the house never gets old...

A long, long driveway flanked on either side of with gigantic hundred-year-old oak trees.

Lush and vibrant in Spring... cool and shady in Summer... bare naked in Winter... and right now?

Spectacular!

Gold, orange and red Autumn leaves as far as the eye can see, falling to the ground as you watch...

After what seems like forever driving through paddocks of fat, shiny black cows and a few handsome horses with their winter pyjamas on, the homestead appears.

Edwardian red clinker bricks with dark green gables.

A grand, beautifully symmetrical one-story heritage home. Imposingly tall but narrowish windows and a wide, tessellated verandah strategically designed to keep the harsh sun at bay. Surrounded by the footprint of the original formal garden - clipped box hedges, standard roses, huge pots of lavender and gardenia - but now a little softer, wilder around the edges.

Danh - who isn't easily impressed - raises his eyebrows and makes a little *Hmmmph!* noise under his breath.

Three cars are parked on the side of the sweeping circular driveway - Grandma's beautiful little 1970 sapphire-blue Pagoda Mercedes convertible... Dad's silver four-door Jag... my brother-in-law Marco's new red family-friendly Alfa SUV...

As we haul ourselves out of the car, two giant black, barking Poodles appear.

Meet Otis and Minka.

For a second they pause to assess the situation, then realising we're all Friendly, they explode with Poodle Joy and jump all over us. Simon and I return their enthusiasm, greeting them like family. Sabine and Danh awkwardly pat their heads in a Good Dog manner.

Then the Poodles notice the Dobermann.

Otis and Nero both stiffen, drawing themselves to maximum height and size each other up cautiously.

Minka starts fan-girling him, darting up to give him a few little kisses. She pauses to assess the likelihood of success should she attempt to steal Gary. Nero looks alarmed and lifting his head to keep Gary out of her reach, gives her wary side-eye.

Giving up on Gary, she zooms off, vanishing from sight before returning a few seconds later with a pinecone in her mouth. She races up to show Nero her treasure, then flies off again, trying to make him chase her.

Nero looks up at me, frowning.

"Yes. She's a lot, but she's harmless. We choose to find it charming..."

Gran appears on the front porch and eagerly beckons us in. Soon we're all being smothered in cosy hugs, whether we like it or not.

She's short, curvy and pretty cool for a Nanna. Not giving in to the years without a fight, her dyed auburn hair shines in the sun and her funky, oversized glasses make her big green eyes even more astonishing.

On this day of saying Thank You, I say Cheers! to Gran for my eyes and my curves...

"Oh Simon! Dear!" she throws her arms around him, pulling him close. There's something soothing and hypnotic about her warm, soft Scottish brogue. "Thank heaven you're alive! Larry told us all about it..."

Given Larry's not one to let the truth limit the potential of a fabulous story, Gran's reaction confirms suspicions that my little sister's version of events has included sirens, flashing lights, defibrillators, angels and at least two near death experiences.

Simon's remarkable People Skills allow him to express gratitude for Gran's concern whilst totally minimising the drama. He is basically a Legend.

She moves on to the surprise guests.

"Sabine dear! How lovely! Don't think we've seen you since you came off Haggis when you were twelve..."

"You got classified Unsafe and I wasn't allowed to visit again..." Sabine grins wryly as she hugs Gran back. "You're looking amazing!"

Haggis is the chestnut demon of a Shetland pony we were all made to learn to ride on. His greatest ability was ejecting small children. Explaining to Mother of Sabine that her cello prodigy daughter had just fallen off a pony and possibly broken her arm can't have been fun...

204

"And you must be Simon's friend...!" as she engulfs Danh, whose eyes widen in alarm. My whole family adores Simon, so unsuspecting Danh is about to be adopted by WASPs - whether he likes it or not.

We follow Gran through the grand-but-pretty stained glass front door and into the wide hallway, me carrying everyone's M-Day flowers and Simon carrying a big box from a fancy bakery. Nero scopes the interior like a security guard. Wary yet thoughtful. The warm walnut wainscoting, antique floorboards and large, round table all shine with love.

"Smells like Old Money..." Danh mutters.

"Not so old... Grandpa's dad was a farmer... who invented a plough-thingy and patented it... which is actually how grandad got interested in law..." I explain, surreptitiously tweaking the pale blue delphiniums in the tall crystal vase on the hall table as we pass.

What once was the ballroom is now a modern family room, with a chef's kitchen, informal dining table and oversized couches perfect for reading in the sunlight or dozing off on. Old School jazz is playing, and the smell of something rich, savoury and complex cooking makes me suddenly realise that I'm starving.

TBJ and Miranda are cooing over tiny baby Grace. Larry is slumped on a chaise, looking very worse for wear as she scrolls half-heartedly. Miranda's husband Marco is at the huge, marble island bench composing an antipasto platter with a level of precision impressive even for an architect... and my dad is next to him concocting a pitcher of cocktails with absolutely no precision at all.

Everybody shrieks *Simon!* and springs toward him, expressing horror, concern and thankfulness for his 'survival'.

Simon once again, accepts the well-wishes with grace before playing it down.

"Oh I'm fine! *Really!* It'll take more than a little bump of some random street drug to keep me out of the game."

Once everyone has sufficiently expressed their relief, they turn their attention to my Extras - Sabine, Danh and a big black dog in a puffer jacket.

"Please tell me that's not my Mother's Day present...?" TBJ asks drily, eying Nero suspiciously.

"Nope! It's just a bunch of 'mums for you!" I laugh, as I hand over her flowers, hugging her. "This is Nero. We're babysitting him for... a friend... who was in a bit of... an accident..."

I'm being deliberately vague, but Dad looks up sharply from pouring vodka. He knows exactly who Nero is, and he seems to know exactly what I'm talking about. Florists may know everything, but when it's Life and Death, there's someone they call even before us...

Their Lawyer.

Visibly relieved she doesn't have to feign *Oh my! I've always wanted a Dobermann*, TBJ holds baby Gracie in her arms and bestows gracious air kisses all round.

She does the meet'n'greet with natural, easy grace. Tall, slim, Golden, stylish and well-preserved. If the house smells like Old Money, my mother looks like it.

However, there's just one thing that's a little odd...

"T-shirt...?" I ask her quizzically.

Now there'd be nothing unusual about her sleek, white Petit Bateau t-shirt and classic dark denims... if it wasn't 13 degrees outside...

"Fucking hormones!" The expletive - possibly the third time in 27 years I've heard her use it - is even more emphatic in her polished

British accent. "My body trying to bloody incinerate itself is getting beyond tiresome."

"*Boop!*" I gently bop Grace's tiny, perfect button nose. Which makes her go cross-eyed. "Golly, she looks just like-"

"Me!" TBJ glows triumphantly.

"I was thinking *Miranda*-"

"Who also looks just like... Me!"

True. Miranda is a Mini Me of Mum... just a smidge taller and a lot less prickly.

"Have you decided on a name yet...?" TBJ *may or may not* have threatened to smother anyone who called her *Grandma* in their sleep...

"I'm quite liking *Babushka*... it sounds a bit glamorous..."

"Not to mention a bit... *Russian*... for a WASP Nanna..." Sabine observes with a wry grin. They don't get any Whiter, more Anglo-Saxon or more Protestant than my mother...

And if there's a Pink Elephant in the room, you can always rely on Sabine to point it out.

"Sabine Darling! Lovely to see you! Not spending the day with your mother...?" Wondering if there's the faintest note of passive-aggression...? Yes, there is, and TBJ is the Master.

208

"An hour of recriminations for my Poor Life Choices over breakfast was enough guilt, thanks!" Sabine smiles, then breaks into a perfect impersonation of her mother. "Sabine! *Oy vey!* Look at you! So thin! Are you on drugs...? What are you doing with your life, Sabine - after all the money we spent on your education??? Why aren't you with the London Philharmonic...??? And where are my grand babies??? Do you want to have a Geriatric Pregnancy??? Is that what you want...?"

Our laughter is interrupted by a softly spoken yet calmly authoritative Scottish accent coming from somewhere in the kitchen.

"Gordon! Do we need to get some tape and mark a line on the floor...? Out! Out of my kitchen! *Now!*"

That's Grandpa... and Dad trying to 'help'.

Our little Mother's Day tradition...

Menfolk do the cooking and the ladies of the house take it easy. Which used to mean Grandpa did everything, until the arrival of Marco and Simon a few years ago...

Marco argued that by virtue of being Italian he is on better terms with food than most people, and sitting in his Nonna's kitchen was enough to learn everything by osmosis. Grandpa - who may or may not be a control freak - has begrudgingly delegated entrée.

Simon - for whom sourcing amazing things is part of his professional skill set - was allowed to find dessert.

Dad has never been trusted with anything more than adult beverages...

Dad appears with a giant pitcher of something thick and blood red with ice, lemon slices and a celery stick.

"Dear God please say that's not just tomato juice, Mr C..." Sabine, apparently, is in need of something to take the edge off.

"It most certainly is not!" grins my Dad, lining up tall glasses. "Who needs some Hair of the Dog...?"

His enthusiasm may exceed his ability in the kitchen, but he mixes a mean cocktail. That his eyes are extra-twinkly and his cheeks are extra-rosy, would suggest that he's been taking quality control very seriously...

Barely average height, stocky and cheeky, he's your typical jovial Scotsman. As a barrister, he basically entertains people for a living and as one of the country's highest paid ones, he's pretty good at it.

"Mangier! Mangier!" and with accompanying theatrical hand gestures, Marco invites us to dig into his very photogenic antipasto.

And *Eat!* is exactly what we do for the next few hours.

A long, leisurely lunch that begins with a delectable selection of charcuterie, cheeses and preserved vegetables, washed down with Dad's deadly Bloody Marys... followed by Grandpa's insanely good 48-hour Beef Bourguignon (with an equally insanely good Pinot Noir from his vineyard) and buttery mashed potatoes...

Relaxed and beautifully informal, we all migrate fluidly around the room...

Sitting on a barstool... leaning on the counter... perching on the arm of a sofa... balancing a bowl in our lap...

Getting caught up with everyone's lives since we last saw each other... gazing through the giant, modern windows and basking in the perfect Autumn day...

Admiring that spectacular view...

Lush, green rolling hills (compete with mob of resident kangaroos grazing and sun-baking) through to wooded mountain ranges in the distance. On the manicured lawn, impossibly tiny brilliant blue wrens - barely bigger than butterflies! - hunt for bugs... flitting, twitching, disappearing then materialising like magic... under a crisp, intense, pale blue sky punctuated with tiny wisps of fluffy white clouds.

So clear, bright and beautiful.

"I shouldn't be drinking *at all* after that party on Friday night..." exclaims TBJ theatrically - though she clearly has absolutely no intention of stopping Marco from refilling her wine glass.

She's talking about the Boa's 50th...

There's not much they don't get invited to, and there's not much they decline... given Dad is fundamentally very social and Mum is fundamentally very nosy. They both would argue *It's good for business* but I think basically they just like to party.

"Was it fun?" I ask hopefully.

"Oh... *Wonderful!* Darling, it was absolutely wonderful! Troy is so clever! We were... *transported!...* And such a beautiful family! Oh, that Ava! She is just *divine...*"

212

Troy??? I'm pretty sure the White Paris thing was pretty much my idea...

But anyway...

"However the magic champagne glass that never emptied did get the better of some of us..." Dad winks cheekily at TBJ. "*Somebody* was speaking French the whole way home and was very sorry for herself in the morning..."

"Hmmmm... those waiters were a bit too diligent on the refill, weren't they...? And such a shame it ended with that whole fracas about Bo's earring..."

Involuntarily I wince.

The earring... the dream...

All true.

The faintest suggestion of a frown clouds Dad's face.

Meanwhile, Miranda has been watching Marco pour wine like a Bloodhound drools over roast chicken.

"I would kill for half a glass... even a sip..." she mutters softly, watching the brilliant ruby-coloured liquid, transfixed.

"How's Parental Leave going...?" I ask, knowing full-well that my perfect, Head Prefect, over-achieving big sister will be going out of her mind playing house all day.

"Well… it's got a bit… *routine*… and Grace is such a good baby… so…"

No idea what's coming next, but can I just say she's barely been away from work a month, and of course Gracie is perfect (because everything in her life just *is*…)

Everyone's conversations have paused and we all wait for Miranda to continue. Intrigued.

"So… Marco and I started looking for a project… and *we think we've found one!*" Her beautiful face lights up and her blue eyes sparkle with excitement.

What…? Where…? everyone asks at once. Her enthusiasm is contagious.

"An old homestead on a sheep station… down on the Shipwreck Coast… We put an offer in last week… *and it was accepted!*" Marco is beaming.

"It's beautiful - or it will be… It's been vacant for sixty years, so it's a huge job… but it's got amazing bones!"

"First job is to convert the stables - so we have somewhere to live… I have so many ideas! My head is…" Marco's fingers do an explosive *BOOM!* at the sides of his crazy, curly hair.

"So the real estate agent was telling buyers the whole property had a heritage overlay and you couldn't do *anything*... and it was full of asbestos... so it's been on the market *forever!*" Miranda exclaims.

"But my little Legal Beagle did some homework and gave him a lesson in Heritage Protection Legislation!" Marco beams with pride at his wife. And he's so earnest, nobody points out that it's actually Eagle, not Beagle...

"And my genius architect husband wasn't afraid of a little asbestos... but there was actually none at all! Winning!"

"1977..." Larry says this to none in particular as she washes a mouthful of mashed potatoes down with a slurp of red. Everyone raises a quizzical eyebrow at her.

"When asbestos was banned in Australia...? Obviously..." Larry explains with her wineglass paused mid-air, unable to entirely hide her frustration this wasn't apparent to everyone else in the room.

Danh stares at her in amazed disbelief. The rest of us are used to it.

"Is she like Pretty Sexy Rainman...?" he whispers.

Yup. Something like that.

"Oh! And don't forget the curse... and the ghosts!" Marco laughs.

Slowly I look up from my plate. As someone who once upon a time could actually see Dead People, this is somewhat disturbing. Okay... so it hasn't happened in years... but the Psychic Mojo is coming back and who knows what it's capable of...???

"But Darling, that's *hours* away!!! How will Marco work...?" TBJ doesn't care about Marco's work. TBJ currently is only fifteen minutes away from Baby Gracie - and wants to keep it that way.

"Oh... most of what I do, I can do remotely..."

Not the answer TBJ was hoping for.

And I'm a bit confused, because I know she's hormonal'n'all, but curtains and colour swatches aren't generally Miranda's idea of a Project.

She's more of a Big Picture girl.

"The out-buildings have so much scope." Miranda's eyes light up. "Stables, cottages, a shearing shed... there's even a chapel! The business opportunities are limitless."

And there you go!

Destination parties and weddings.

There's your Big Picture.

My phone dings... I frown.

Message from Seb Marchesi.

I open it to see a screenshot of Nero's Instagram - a pic from his Gangsta period -

Please Explain.

He looks like Ivan's Spirit Animal...

I splutter my wine, trying to suppress a giggle.

Then right on cue I hear Simon ask-

"Delia, may I borrow this for a second...?"

And before I can ask *borrow what?*, Simon has tied Grandma's floral Liberty print apron around Nero's neck and waist with big, neat bows.

"Can I get your paws up here please...?" Simon gestures to the bench, giving direction like he would to a model. "How about smiling...? Oh... That's Gold!"

Before I can count to ten, my phone dings.

Seb's sent me the reel Simon just shot...

Nero, in apron, positioned behind the bottle and full wineglass, scrunching up his nose to reveal all his brilliant white teeth in a spectacular grin and wishing everyone a Happy Mother's Day.

SEB *Seriously???*

ME *Puppers have mothers too...?*

He doesn't reply, but I can see him shaking his head.
Hopefully he's doing okay...

The menfolk have spirited all the dirty dishes away to the butlers pantry. Grandpa reappears and looks around expectantly.

"Right! Who's coming for a walk...?" he asks.

It's actually a rhetorical question, because we all either want to see the beautiful grounds, or physically need to move to make room for dessert.

We head out to the garden via the Mud Room - a narrow corridor neatly lined with coats, all manner of hats and boots. I pull on my petrol blue parka, fair isle beanie and camouflage print gum-boots.

Simon's eyes light up and he grabs Grandpa's quilted field vest, a tweed newsboy cap and a dark green tartan scarf... which he artfully arranges on Nero. Grabbing some gloves and secateurs (because you never know when you'll have to chop something...) from a big wicker basket, I shake my head.

"You're out of control..." I mutter to Simon as I pass him.

"I know, right?"

And we walk. The air is cold, clean and crisp, but the sun is gloriously warm. The green lawns are scattered with leaves in every shade of gold, copper and red. As the summer flowers shut down for winter, the camellias are covered in buds. It's almost their time to shine. In the surrounding paddocks, row upon row of grapevine stands almost naked. They'll all need to be cut back, but not just yet.

When we were at school, Miranda was the Sporty One. Larry was the Musical/Theatrical One. And I had no apparent extra-curricular talents. Other than a way with animals and plants. So while they spent their weekends playing tournaments and at lessons or re-hearsals, I went to the Farm with my grandparents.

And I loved every minute of it.

We do a leisurely lap of the home paddocks. The Poodles keep flying off ahead of us in excitement, then circle back and wait impatiently for us to catch up. Nero stays close to his people, observing everything. Calm, but alert.

"Hey Lil' Humphrey!" I call out to a glossy Aberdeen Angus bull. I helped hand rear him when his mother tragically died. He was tiny but he was a fighter. He now weighs close to a tonne, but he'll always be Little to me. Humphrey regards the cluster of people suspiciously. He loves me and Grandma, tolerates Grandpa... and would happily trample anyone else to death. I hang back as they head over to the stables.

When they're sufficiently gone, he trots up to the fence and nuzzles his giant head into my chest, covering my parka in grassy cow snot and nearly knocking me over.

I trace my fingers around the whorl of hair on his broad fore-head - a perfect spiral right between his eyes - over and over until he goes cross-eyed, his ears blissfully melting backwards to slide down his neck.

Abruptly he looks up with a start and a wary snort. The ground reverberates as his back hoof agitatedly strikes the ground.

"He never did like sharing you..." Dad chuckles, wryly.

"He doesn't have to..." I reply, massaging his ears to placate him. "He is the only man in my life."

"Interesting you should say that, because a most curious rumour came to me whilst minding my own business this week..." His voice is light and his face is neutral, but his eyes are watching my face very carefully.

"How very unusual..." I say this with irony, because Dad isn't adverse to a bit of scuttlebutt... because where there's smoke, there's fire... and where's there's fire, there's people scrambling for a lawyer...

"A little bird told me that one of my daughters is having an affair with a very prominent, very married man..."

Oh shit!

Somebody knows about Ash Knight and Larry... How could they be so stupid??? *This is BAD!*

And I realise too late that I should have put on my best game face, because Dad reads faces for a living... and he's just seen the

little tornado of emotions in mine... and he knows he's onto something.

"And here, indeed, is my middle daughter... with Sebastian
Marchesi's dog... seemingly very familiar with very private details of
his life... Is there something you'd like to tell me?"

And you know what's the first thing that pops into my head...?

Cluedo!

Cressida. In the kitchen. With the Dobermann.

A little splutter of nervous giggles escape quite involuntarily.

Of relief, that Larry maybe isn't quite busted... yet...

Of the sheer ridiculousness of me having an affair with Seb Marchesi...

And the mental picture of cartoon Me, in an orange retro cocktail dress (with matching slingbacks and fascinator) holding carton
Nero by a giant black leather studded collar...

Then I start shaking my head incredulously.

No.

Oh *Good God no!!!*

I'm not the Mystery Mistress!

Somebody's barking up the right tree, but the wrong rat... And
the wrong daughter...

But there *is* something I've been putting off telling him... here we go... I breathe in very slowly and exhale loudly to prepare myself.

"I don't know how to say this, but-"

"Oh dear..." he murmurs sadly, looking almost heart-broken. His worst suspicion confirmed. You can almost see his brain start running damage control strategies.

"Oh no! Not *that*! I would never do that! I've... started having dreams... like Gran..."

"Oh dear!!!" he murmurs again, this time emphatic and alarmed. Also disturbing and problematic... but in a whole different way.

"I saw the Cayenne get pushed off the cliff. I called it in. I possibly saved his life... Crazy, huh...?"

"Did you just say *pushed*...?" he pounces. He's trying to keep his poker face on, but he's clearly perturbed.

"Yup. A dark Range Rover. Lined him up and flicked him

right over the edge... so why is he trying to minimise it...? I know they're going to try again."

Dad frowns. Marchesi is his client. I search his face, looking for clues. How much has Seb told him...?

How much does he know...?

"It's a blessing you saved his life, but you need to leave it be now. Sebastian Marchesi is a man of resource and talent. He can take care of himself. I need you to promise me you'll do that, Trouble. Please...?"

I make a non-comital *mmmmm* noise, whilst nodding and shaking my head at the same time... like toddlers do when they try to tell a lie.

"Does your mother know?" After *Is there something you'd like to tell me?* , the second most popular question in his Daughter Cross Examination repertoire.

I shake my head.

"Let's just leave it that way for now, shall we...? Janey doesn't embrace the... esoteric... like us Carlisles do..."

I nod in agreement, very happy to avoid that conversation for the time being. I got enough goin' on, without TBJ on my case.

"When did this start...?"

"My birthday... Gran said something big was going to happen..."

"She's never wrong!" shaking his head in admiration and amazement. He clears his throat. "I owe you an apology. I know you have more character - and intelligence - than to put yourself in that situation... and it obviously isn't Miranda... and it would never be my little Larry!"

"Oh no! Never Larry." The words - delivered with the tiniest drizzle of sarcasm - are out of my mouth before I can stop them. Fortunately he doesn't seem to notice the tone, or consider all the other prominent, married men in Melbourne with dodgy moral compasses it could potentially be...

We join the rest of our party. Larry is perched on a stable door, pulling pouty faces as she tries to snuggle into a handsome bay gelding for a selfie. TBJ, who believes there are no coincidences, only opportunities, is grilling Danh about how to up her 'mature age' make up game.

"Take the contour above the crease, right up the bone - I know, it feels wrong, but you'll be amazed how it lifts and opens the eye..."

And Danh seems happy and relieved to be able to talk about something that's in his wheelhouse.

Grandpa has baby Gracie balanced nonchalantly on one fore-arm. Animals and babies... they all love Grandpa. They gaze ador-ingly at each other while he discusses jazz with Sabine (he used to play clarinet).

Gran is brutally pruning a rose, as Miranda and Marco inundate her with Garden Questions in preparation for their new project.

"You can't kill a rose, dear... it's quite impossible..." as she man-ically hacks away, reducing the bush to a handful of short, naked sticks. I pull on the gardening gloves and get stuck into its neighbour. Cutting back the new growth... removing branches that cross over... relieving it of any dead wood and stems 'thinner than a pencil'... just like she taught me.

When it's time to head back to the house for dessert, I fall in step with her.

"Yes, Dear...?" I guess she doesn't have to be particularly psy-chic to figure out there's something I need to ask her.

I take a very deep breath, frowning.

Because I really don't know where to begin...

"Start with the big picture, Dear... then the little things will all make sense..." Gran suggests helpfully.

"How can you tell when you've got it right... and when your instincts are wrong...?"

"Your instincts are always right, dear. Trust them."

"But yesterday I got something pretty much wrong..."

"But did you...?"

Errrr... yep. I'm pretty sure I did. Wrong person ended up in the ambulance.

"How do you know it wasn't your instincts, but *the reality* that turned out wrong...?" and with thoughtfully raised eyebrows and an intriguing little smile, she leaves me to ponder her hypothetical riddle.

Fortunately, my brain is saved from going around and around Larry-Simon-Skeletor loop like a dog chasing its tail...

My phone dings with a message. I look at it and giggle.

MARCHESI So

My dog now has more followers than I do???

ME I can give u his stylist's number if u like

MARCHESI Thank you for helping out.

I appreciate it

Ivan can take him now

Drop off at St Francis - when suits?

I work out how long the little detour will take on the way home and text him back. He sends Ivan's number, with instructions to let him know when we're ten minutes out.

Stepping inside, we're greeted with the heavenly smell of hot, sweet, apple and cinnamon baked goods. Grandpa removes the pie from the oven with a flourish, then carefully pours his creme anglaise into a pretty crystal jug. Any breathing room in our bellies quickly vanishes.

Dad offers coffee to the responsible grown-ups, and a dram of single malt to the irresponsible ones. Then suggests the third option of whisky *in* the coffee, for those shooting for the appearance of respectability.

We say our goodbyes, groaning and bemoaning the state of our struggling digestive systems.

228

The parents, grandparents, Larry and Team Miranda are all driving home tomorrow. Dad has two brothers overseas who'll call 'home' when New York and London wake up.

"You're most welcome to stay, dears!" Gran offers kindly. "There's plenty of food and enough beds for you all..."

I'm just about to reply that I have an early start tomorrow when...

"Thank you so much - we'd love to, but we already have plans for tonight!" Simon sounds very excited.

"What's tonight...?" I ask, wracking my sleep-deprived brain.

Nope. I got nothing.

My plans for tonight involve a toasty warm bed, a fluffy pillow and at least ten hours of (hopefully) uninterrupted sleep.

"You're kidding me???" Simon is completely incredulous. "No. Seriously. You *are* joking, right...?"

I press my lips together, shaking my head.

No. I am not.

"*Eurovision Party!* At Karmageddon. *Fancy... Dress... Eurovision... Party...* Remember...? Prize for Best Costume...?"

Oh shit! Yes I do.

And oh shit! I was supposed to get a costume.

At the mention of *Karmageddon*, Lovely Larry who had been lounging half-asleep on the chaise, springs to life.

"Oooh! I love Eurovision! Can I come?"

"How *anyone* can love Eurovision beggars belief..." mutters TBJ with an eyeroll. Sabine nods in enthusiastic agreement.

"Seriously! Can I come too...? I really want to go!" Larry is like a dog with a bone.

I narrow my eyes at her. The promise of possibly bumping into Ash Knight is why she wants to go to Karmageddon...

I remember my crazy dream from last night and vaguely wonder if this is a good idea...

But that was just a dream, right...?

"Are you in...?" I ask Sabine. I know she's probably about to be spirited to somewhere hip and exciting again... I feel like I've hardly seen her...

"Oh... I'd rather eat glass... but for you, I will do it..." she replies dramatically. "But I'm so *not* doing fancy dress!"

I hug the parents, the grandparents and Marco goodbye.

"Love you like a rainbow!" I say softly and sweetly, giving baby Gracie one last boop on her tiny little nose.

Miranda reaches out with her free arm, slipping it around my neck to pull my cheek up to her lips.

She plants a smoochie kiss, then murmurs …

"Love *you* like a rainbow! And can we talk wedding flowers sometime…"

"I'm pretty sure you guys already did that…?"

"Not me! The farm. Some ballpark costings… wedding bouquets… chapel flowers… decorating the shearing shed…"

"Given you essentially have me in a headlock… yes, we can."

"*Correct answer!*" smiles Golden Girl down at me triumphantly. "Tuesday's your day off…? I'll send through some photos for reference, then I'll call you at 11."

And being the glorious triumph of Type A perfection that she is, you know she will…

So… with one extra body in the tiny Mercedes, what was 'cosy' on the way down is positively squooshy on the way home. Simon, Sabine and Larry are wedged into the back seat. Nero is crammed in at my feet in the front passenger seat, sitting uncomfortably be-tween my legs and trying to lean his chin on the armrest. Gary sits in my lap, facing forward and watching anxiously where we're going.

We head back to civilisation in the fading light.

By the time we pull up out the front of the hospital, it's dark.

Ivan is waiting for us. He and Nero nod a business-like *Hello* at each other, then Ivan attempts to figure out what looks like the Kev-lar version of a very complicated dog harness.

"May I...?" I interject, politely pointing out which bit goes where. Years of helping Gran put bridles, saddles and rugs on horses makes it easy for me to make sense of it.

There are big, red letters embroidered on each side. SERVICE DOG.

"I didn't know he was a Service Dog..." I exclaim.

"He is now!" Ivan replies, a little smugly.

I carefully tuck Gary through the padded handle on top. Ivan discreetly slips something into my hand.

A roll of notes.

"Thank you. Mr Marchesi very grateful to you... *Hey!* What you doing???"

Nero has puffed himself up to full magnificence, and is staring fixedly into the plate glass windows of the hospital foyer.

"I think he's checking himself out..." I giggle, because Nero is, indeed, striking a pose and admiring his own reflection.

"You supposed to be guard dog, remember...?" Ivan shakes his head and rolls his eyes. "Yes, you very, very handsome man... now come on! Watch dog needs to *watch!*"

He claps his hands and Nero snaps to attention.

I wave goodbye and Nero gives me a conspiratorial little nod, as Ivan clips an unnecessary lead onto his collar.

And together they march into the hospital foyer, preparing to report for duty.

It's a small world, after all...

Three hours later, and we're being dropped at the end of an inner-city laneway. Now usually this would mean we're in the Karmageddon home straight, however with tonight's footwear ranging from Precarious to Potentially Fatal, the uneven bluestone laneway and the seven flights of stairs add a diabolical degree of difficulty to reaching our destination.

Simon and Danh, plus photographer Dave, fashion designer Jimmy Quan and prosthetic make-up expert Martin are paying their very authentic respects to Scandinavian Death Metal (*Eurovision Male Look #9 - We're In League With Satan*). Black jeans and black t-shirts adorned with elaborate moulded shoulder pads and cod pieces that Martin has expertly created to look like they're fashioned from dragon skin. Horns appear to be erupting on their foreheads - also Martin's handiwork. Ashen skin... face tatts... black eyes... black lips. Their customarily very cool hair is random and disheveled.

"How do we look...?" Simon asked with a grin.

"Profoundly disturbing!" I replied.

"I know, right...? We are *so* fucking winning!"

But the *piece de resistance* is the footwear.

Black leather platform ankle boots covered with a prosthetic cloven hoof.

Now... if you've ever tried to negotiate cobblestones in platforms, you understand one thing...

It is fraught with danger! There is much swearing, stumbling and staggering as our little baby dragons try to make their way to the 12 foot tall mural of Kali the Destroyer, who guards the front door.

After Simon's initial freakout at my lack of costume, he got straight on the job as soon as we climbed into the car to head home. As a stylist, he gets thrown curve-balls all the time, so he's Grace Under Pressure, so to speak...

He hit up Jimmy Quan and it went something like this...

"Hey... I need to dress three girls for tonight -"

"*Two!* You need to dress *two* girls. Sabine doesn't do 'costume', remember...?" Sabine interjects.

"Bah! That's no fun at all... So Jimmy! My favourite Fashion Guru... hiding in your glorious archives are there a few of your more 'theatrical' babies that would love a night out...? For Cressida and her sister, Larry..."

He rattles off our heights, weights and measurements.

"That's... ridiculous!" exclaims Larry. I'm guessing from her amazed wonder, he's right on the money with her Vital Statistics.

"...and matching shoes, sizes eight and six, if poss..."

Jimmy came through with a selection of awe-inspiring (and not in a good way) treasures.

I was squeezed into an obscenely short little number... in purple lurex... with only one sleeve... that is so puffed up at the shoulder, it's bigger than my head... if this isn't already *extra* enough, the sleeve extends over my hand to hook onto my middle finger like an Evil Queen in a Disney musical. If this doesn't already scream *Eurovision Girl Look #4 - The Kooky Architectural Dress*, there's the magnificent accordion pleated cape that cascades down the back and attaches at the wrist of the sleeve. The look is completed with perilously high black suede over-the-knee boots.

As my hair was backcombed, then smoothed into a comically grand French roll... my eyes were made very dark and smouldering, and my lips very red... and Simon turned a silver chainmail snake bangle into an earring to decorate my one naked shoulder... I contemplated my fate for the evening...

A hemline to short to sit down and heels to high to stand up... It possibly should have been obvious that this wasn't going to be a great idea...

Larry was all but muttering *My Precious!* as she snatched a spectacular gown best described as Naked Mermaid - and *Eurovsion Girl Look #3 - Slutty Princess.* Full-length, backless, split to the navel at the front... in stretchy flesh-tone fabric covered with tiny crystals... completed with a theatrical fishtail hem and monster stiletto lucite platform sparkly sandals that any pole dancer would kill for...

Danh did peachy, luminous makeup with some subtle glitter, then artfully shaded pink hairspray over the mid-lengths and ends of her long golden-brown through to blonde ombre hair. No prizes for guessing who she's hoping will be there...

"Just whenever you're ready..." Sabine calls out, bored and a little condescending, waiting impatiently at the doorway. She conceded to the addition of a beret and sassy neck kerchief as Danh pinned her hair into a chic chignon, which took her stripy jumper, hip jeans and Adidas Sambas from looking a bit French to perfectly Parisian.

It also made her the only member of our party still able to walk normally and not like a new born foal...

Shuddering with cold, I finally arrive at Kali the Destroyer. Sparkly purple architectural dress has the additional problem that you can't get a coat over that crazy puffy sleeve. I glance up at Kali's magnificent blue body, complete with ten arms holding an arsenal of weapons and a severed male head. The door handle is cleverly disguised as the handle of her knife. Inside the huge, open stairwell climbing the seven flights of worn bluestone stairs, it's sadly barely warmer than outside.

Finally... we fling the doors open onto the sensory overload that is Karmageddon. Taking its cue from a Rajasthani palace, it is a riot of colour, texture and noise. No surface has been overlooked.

The walls are covered with elaborate mirrors, cheeky Indian-inspired paintings and murals, ranging from Marharajas to the Karma Sutra (which induces a little panic attack... you'll see why sooner or later...)

Grand, tessellated and painted columns... gigantic, lavishly up-holstered couches around ornate carved wood coffee tables... wild oriental carpets...

Tonight there's a monster screen displaying the Eurovision broadcast, and we're greeted with tv commentary, instead of the usual celebrity DJ banging out a too cool for school mix of tunes. And instead of looking inspiringly Super Hip, the crowd looks like giant primary schoolers celebrating Book Week.

We scan the vast room, looking for friends... hopefully who have snaffled a couch or two... and *Bingo!*

Simon starts waving at two sassy Cossacks in hot pants, who are valiantly trying to keep possession of two couches as various groups circle like sharks. A very relived looking Indigo from Vogue (who you met at the Thirsty Dog last night... and I'm guessing that's the fur hat Ava's wearing on this month's front cover)... and Eloise the Account-ant (who Simon met on a plane once)...

Simon's curiosity, thoughtfulness and very genuine interest in people means he collects new Best Friends like a highly sociable tod-dler.

I head to the packed bar to get our first round. Drinks are on Mr Marchesi tonight... Cheers Seb!

The staff are all dressed like it's Oktoberfest *(Eurovision Look #1 - Cheeky Homage to National Costume)*. My feet are already starting to burn, so I'm hoping this won't take any longer than it has to... We party here quite a lot, and they also get Le Jardin flowers quite regularly, so I'm trying to catch the eye of someone I know when a loud voice is in my ear...

"Nice dress! Hey!... I need you!!!"

I turn to see a tall guy with a smooth, boyish face who I suspect is older than he looks. He's wearing a white dress shirt and tuxedo pants. The sleeves are rolled up and sitting under the unbuttoned collar is an undone bow tie. *Eurovision Male Look #3... The Tortured Romantic.*

"I'm pretty sure you don't and I'm quite positive it's not mutual." Interfering with a girl trying to get an adult beverage. Grave tactical error, Mate.

"But I do! We are the perfect duet!" is his confident and completely unfazed reply, gesturing to our respective outfits like it should be very obvious.

He's not going to give up, is he...?

"And what are we going to sing...?" I ask, perhaps a tad patron-isingly, humouring him.

"Oh I feel it should be angsty... very angsty..." he replies earnestly.

"Did you cheat on me, perhaps...?" Because he *does* look like the cheating kind...

"Oh no... more can't live with you, can't live without you kind of thing..." as he waves his hands in an expressive, theatrical manner.

"I'm pretty sure U2 already did that..." trying to be politely dismissive, but he's not one for taking hints.

"So what's your name? I should know that , if we're going to be partners... Mine's Grant."

Persistent, much...?

"Hi Grant! I'm-"

"It's *Gra-ah-nt*, not Grant."

He pronounces his name with an exaggeratedly long, affected and kinda whiny *aaah* sound.

I search behind the bar in vain for somebody to take my money and rescue me from this conversation.

"Hello Gra-aaah-nt. I'm Cressida."

"So... who are you here with?"

Direct, much...?

"Over there... Satan's Baby Dragons, Barbie Cossacks, Catherine Deneuve and the mermaid..."

"I'm just here with my staff."

"And what do you do that necessitates staff, Gr-aaaah-nt...?"

"I'm *Graahnt Ransom!.*" He says this like it should mean something to me. "I made this a team building exercise."

I look politely blank. If you live in this town and I don't know who you are, you're either not as successful as you like to think you are... or you don't send flowers...

"GG Inc...?"

That vaguely rings a bell, but I still got nothing.

"Mercenary. The game. I made it... amongst others..."

Fortunately I'm saved from feigning further interest as the bar staff finally get to me. I yell out my order as I pull the giant roll of notes Ivan gave me from my sleeve.

"And you are apparently a drug dealer..." he observes.

"Oh no! I just did a favour for a friend."

"Who's a drug dealer..."

"Oh God no... I'm pretty sure I don't know any drug dealers..."

Hmmm... pretty... sure...?

"Hey! I'll come over and find you later..."

I nod vaguely, strongly suspecting that he will do exactly that, as I return to my peeps with as many glasses as possible clutched in one hand... and a giant pitcher of black, red and gold horizontally striped rocket fuel, in honour of the host country, Germany.

Packed room, tiny disco-ball dress, lethal heels plus glasses and violently coloured beverage made the Degree of Difficulty for crossing the room a solid 9.5. I've almost made it back to the safety of our sofas when I once again hear those fateful words...

"Hey! Nice dress!"

I've been so focussed on my motor skills, I hadn't even noticed I was about to walk smack-bang into a very Green Rory. And I've been so focussed on everything else, I completely forgot I was supposed to be meeting him here. Don't know why the Chinese proverb *A crisis is an opportunity riding a dangerous wind* suddenly springs to mind...

"It's got nothin' on your hat..." I reply with a smirk.

Rory's taken Team Ireland literally and has gone full soccer hooligan - jersey, scarf, giant green leprechaun hat, Irish flag painted on each cheek.

Holding up the splendid multi-coloured jug, I raise a sassy eyebrow at him.

"Ready...?" I ask expectantly.

"Born ready!" he replies with a grin, producing his own empty glass and carefully extracting one for me from the collection in my hand. He holds the glasses steady while I attempt to pour.

We say *Cheers!* as Rory clinks our glasses together.

"To Ireland!" Rory raises his glass in a toast to his mother country, then slams its contents down the hatch.

He raises the other glass to my lips.

"Ready...? On three..." and after counting to three, he carefully tips it into my mouth. "Now that wasn't so bad, was it...?"

"The actual drink is terrible!" I exclaim. "But the process was not too bad at all... Hey! Can I ask you a question...?"

"Go for it!" he asks enthusiastically. Intrigued.

"Are you wearing trainers? Because if you are, I am seriously so envious of you right now... I chose *really* freaking badly!" I confess, a little mournfully.

"Yes I am. If you need a hand getting down the stairs, I'm happy to be your knight in shining armour."

"Good to know."

The way my feet are howling, I might just be taking him up on that...

"And what the fuck is that...?" Sabine eyes pitcher with suspicion as I set it triumphantly on our coffee table.

"Ummm... Germany in a jug...?" The only bit I remember is red vodka...

She rolls her dark, dark brown eyes and reluctantly accepts a glass.

"Oh! Guess who says Hi...?" she asks with cheeky grin.

"Who???"

"That is not guessing..."

"C'mon... *who???* I will point out that I know where you're ticklish..."

"Well you're no fun at all..." she sighs, then she pauses expectantly for dramatic impact... "Tomcat Hardy!"

Tom Hardy is the lead singer of supergroup Seven - and the sexiest man on the planet. Simon worked with them on a video about a month ago and introduced me to Tom... who was apparently flirting with me, but I was either too drunk or too clueless to realise...

"How funny is that…?" I ask, meaning funny as in unusual, not funny amusing. Actually I'm pretty astonished he remembered me at all.

"Funny…? A rock god says to say Hi… and you think it's… *funny?*… Seriously, is it any wonder you're single…?"

Sabine pauses for a mouthful of German flag, pulls a face and shakes her head at the disturbing flavour profile, and is preparing to launch into Round 2 of Cressida Is Romantically Rubbish.

Vaguely I wonder if I should get that on a coffee mug…

Is it any wonder I'm single…?

Then I have a flashback to my chat with the Tomcat…

"And how's Matt?" I ask pointedly, with a sly raised eyebrow.

You see, I'm not the only one who needs the coffee mug…

For a split second, her dark, dark brown eyes look so pained, I feel bad I went there.

Then streetwise, unsinkable Sabine is back in the room.

"The relationship was unviable." Her reply is calm and matter-of-fact.

"That's a very *scientific* adjective for a very hot thing…" I observe quietly.

Matt is the bass player in supergroup, Seven. Sabine played 'cello on their last studio album... Tomcat told me she messed with him. Big time. And from the look on Sabine's face, the messing was very mutual.

"How does it work...???" she asks softly. Almost plaintively. "Half the time we're not even on the same continent, let alone the same time zone... He's not quitting Seven and I'm not quitting my career to follow him on tour like some sad Groupie girlfriend..."

I give her tanned wrist an empathetic squeeze, trying to think of a solution to her Sexy Cello Girl problems, when my laboured thought process is interrupted by a voice very close, right in my ear. The hispanic accent gives the *s* sounds the faintest lisp.

"Hey Flower Girl! Nice dress!!!"

I turn to see the very handsome face of Karmageddon's Chilean manger, Diego. Warm, dark eyes and warm smile. Perfectly manscaped moustache and beard. Longish dark hair set in waves like a '30s movie star.

And a full-length, sequinned lilac chiffon gown.

"Nice dress to you too!" I laugh.

"Hi! I'm Cressida's sister, Larry!" and with her most engaging smile, Lovely Larry appears out of nowhere and insinuates herself into the conversation. "Is Ash around...?"

I raise a *Really???* eyebrow at her, before she smoothly carries on...

"We were talking on Friday at the Marchesi job... he said he'd be interested in seeing my CV..."

"You can just flick it to me and I'll pass it on," Diego offers helpfully (although not remotely helpful for Larry...) "Ash is down the coast with his wife's family this weekend. He wants to buy Angelica a beach house for her birthday. They'll be judging the costumes though... we're posting pics on Insta..."

Not what Lovely Larry wanted to hear... she murmurs a polite Thank You, but looks disappointed and deflated as she disappears into the crowd.

And Diego turns his attention back to me.

"Have you seen the —" he breaks off the sentence and gestures with his head over to the hallway which leads to the restrooms.

"No. No I have not." I reply a little curtly, as butterflies of dread and anticipation unfurl their wings in my stomach.

"Now that hurts my feelings!" he smiles as he feigns offence. "Actually, I think it's one of my favourites..."

Diego is also a crazy talented illustrator. He's responsible for all the amazing artworks... and probably most of the better tattoos in here.

"Nobody can tell it's me, right...?"

"No, they can't. Don't worry - you're safe!" he replies reassuringly. "I always put a few clues in, but unless you're really looking for it, you can't -"

His sentence is interrupted by the arrival of a tall girl with a crazy-fit body in a baby blue unitard. Dark hair slicked back, dramatic makeup.

"The photo booth's empty if some of these guys want to jump in..." she politely interjects. Noticing me looking a little quizzically at her costume, she breaks out the Jazz Hands, then busts a few crazy neck rolls and high kicks. "It wouldn't be Eurovision without interpretive dance... I have a troupe. We've been practicing. We're winning Best Group."

"You're not competing. Remember...? We talked about this..." Diego gets a bit agitated and starts sounding a lot more Hispanic than his customary calm professional self.

"Why not? We want to win!"

"Perhaps because you're *my wife*...? Which means it's really not appropriate, is it...?"

Meet Diego's beautiful (if somewhat unhealthily competitive) wife, Jess.

"I would love for you guys to perform while I'm announcing the winners - wouldn't that be amazing...?" And after successfully placating her, Diego switches to Manager Mode and raises his voice so everyone can hear him. "Best Female, Best Male, Best Gender Fluid, Best Duet and Best Group... a $500 bar tab for the winner of each category. Judged by Ash and Angelica on Photo Booth performance, so make it good!"

We hurry over to the Photo Booth before anyone else beats us to it. Sabine waves us away as she promises to guard our spot.

With dozens of digital backdrops, microphones, instruments and a bizarre assortment of props, it is truly next level.

The Baby Dragons choose a melodramatic galaxy background that's all inky, purply black with exploding stars and molten lava. Simon stands on the bass drum, and they all scream angrily whilst either smashing or licking guitars.

Then it's my turn. I'm scrolling through my backdrop options, when a largish hand reaches in front of me to click on one.

"That's it! Darkness, spotlights, smoke. Perfect! And I'm thinking *these*..."

For the second time that evening, I turn to look up at that very irritating man-child in half a tuxedo... who is right now holding a pair of microphones that are completely covered in twinkling crystals.

"You're not going to go away, are you..."

"Nope. I've scouted the talent. The Duet category is looking pretty soft and you're my best chance of winning it."

I look at him incredulously - and realise that he is deadly serious. He hands me a microphone.

"Hey - 250 bucks is 250 bucks, right...? So let's just get up there and belt something out like we really mean it!"

I guess it's a lot less embarrassing than doing it alone... and he has a point about the 250 bucks...

There's just one thing I need to sort out...

"Can I ask you a question...?"

"Shoot!" he replies eagerly.

"You're wearing novelty socks, aren't you...?" I ask him, completely deadpan.

"Not what I was expecting... but, yes..."

After a split-second of confused surprise, he recovers and leans over to raise the hem of his pants. Martini glasses and green olives on toothpicks...

"I like to match my socks to the occasion."

And are we surprised...?

Oh no. We are not.

And now that we've got that out of the way, let's get on with it!

"So what are we singing...? I feel we need something Max Angst..." I ask him. Given he apparently has this all figured out.

"*Creep*... the She Runs bit. Nothing angstier than that... And make it convincing! I'm here to win."

So we walk onto our little set.

Safe in the knowledge that with Eurovision blaring plus all the raucous bar noise nobody will be able to hear us scream, I belt out the bridge from Creep like my life depends on it.

We are so getting into it, we incorporate a few diva moves and theatrical head tosses. As the last note ends, I finish with a melodramatic look away from Gr-aaah-nt. There's a burst of spontaneous applause from everyone waiting.

"C'mon... admit it... that was fun. Right...?" Grant enthuses as he takes the mic off me. "Let's get a drink to celebrate our inevitable victory!"

"Admirable as your optimism is, I need to help my sister with her photo..."

"Okay. Later then. I'll find you."

Yup. I do not doubt that for a minute.

In actuality, Lovely Larry could not be any less in need of assistance. With a decisive click she chooses a delicate, hazy, rainbow background and grabs a simple acoustic guitar.

Perching herself gracefully on a tall stool that shows off her spectacular sparkly dress and sexy sandals, she arranges her long,

254

pink mermaid locks so they cascade over one shoulder, checks out her very visible cleavage and expertly places her hands on the strings…

And… *she starts playing!!!*

A beautiful progression of gentle, melancholy chords. *And then she starts singing!*

A soft, sad, sweet song in a warm, husky, melodic voice. She looks up at the camera through her fluttery eyelashes, shyly but a little slyly, with a charmingly mysterious Mona Lisa smile… sweetly vindictive in the knowledge that her lover and his wife are going to see her look perfectly rapturous.

"*Omfg!* I never knew Larry could sing! I never knew she could play guitar!" Simon is incredulous.

"*I* never knew either! Nobody did…" I shrug, equally incredulous.

And the next hour passes in a relaxed, irreverent blur.

With much eye-rolling from Sabine, we watch excitedly as the Grand Final of the Eurovision Music Festival unfolds. The good, the bad, the kitsch and the cringe-worthy. Everything from Boy Bands, to Black Tie crooners, to babes in bikinis. Suddenly everyone is an expert on Euro pop culture... and European relations.

Oh God no! They'd never vote for Armenia...

Pics from the Photo Booth have been uploaded on their Insta, and I have to say we all look pretty damn fabulous. Larry is cocooned in a corner of the couch, her drink resting precariously on the arm... texting... the speed of her thumbs increasing with her escalating emotions.

No prizes for guessing who's on the other end of that...

The music goes quiet and Diego appears on the little stage in front of the screen. He begins talking - welcoming us, thanking us for our enthusiasm, telling us how great we all look - with Jess and co hilariously translating his words into highly creative interpretive dance moves.

And as I realise everyone in the building is right now gathered expectantly in this room, waiting eagerly for the announcement of the winners of 500 bucks, I'm thinking it's probably not a bad time to go look at *that*.

Surreptitiously (or as surreptitiously as one can wearing a purple disco ball) I slip out to the deserted hallway.

Doors to the fire escape at one end, restrooms at the other.

And somewhere in between is a funny little alcove... that now houses a larger than life apparently naked portrait of me... suspended upside down... my butt nestled in an apparently naked man's lap... the soles of my feet resting on his impressive chest... his strong arms supporting me...

Ladies and Gentleman, may I present *The Trapeze!*

I stare, transfixed, first in fascinated horror. Then, as I realise it's such an obliquely referenced Bollywood caricature that nobody's going to recognise me, I begin to appreciate and admire it.

It's sassy, sexy and charming.

We appear to be having an absolute ball, laughing with wild abandonment. I look for Diego's three clues... instantly the luminous green eyes hit me... the flowers strewn all over the romantic bed and the rug... delicate, exotic, bright flowers... and the third...? My tangerine toenails!

I smile. It's actually pretty cool.

Who's the guy...? He's one of Jess' PT clients and he's posed for a bunch of them. Though I'd already met him the day before... he's one of the Special Ops guys who saved me from a dungeon on a psycho serial killer's super yacht (but that's another story for another day...). Anyways, he was an absolute legend.

Polite, respectful and made me feel as relaxed as one possibly can whilst hanging upside-down, wearing nothing but skin-tone bum-huggers. And just as I'm wondering if Lachlan/Tex has seen it yet, an electric jolt of panic goes through my whole body.

Larry!

Something's about to happen to Larry...

Frantically I look around the corner of the alcove to see a flash of crystals and pastel pink hair at the other end of the long hallway. She's frowning at her phone... and I can faintly hear her repeatedly saying *Hello...?* in a hushed, urgent voice... becoming increasingly agitated and frustrated.

She is so focused on her phone, she doesn't notice the fire escape door quietly open and two guys in black hoodies appear.

I stand frozen in horror as they creep up behind her, hovering... like they're waiting for... *that!*

She stumbles.

The phone slips from her fingers.

She looks around, disorientated.

She crumples like a rag doll.

The taller one clamps a hand calmly over her mouth. They catch her body as it slumps towards the ground. They drag her body to the fire door and open it.

And suddenly the dream replays in my head...

I see Larry's limp body sailing past the Karmageddon windows to splatter on the street below...

"LARRY!!!" I scream it louder than I even knew I could. Her name echoes through the deserted corridor. A panic-stricken, hysterical shriek.

Her attackers pause, startled. The tall, skinny one looks me right in the eye.

Every fibre of my being prickles with recognition.

Skeletal face. Teardrop tattoo. Lips parted in an expressionless grimace.

Then they urgently resume dragging her limp body through the doorway.

Frantically I look around in vain for help.

There is no one.

It's all up to me.

Somehow... despite ridiculous heels and absurdly short, tight dress... I run... faster than I knew I ever could... screaming with all my lungs...

"LARRY!!! HELP!!! SOMEBODY... PLEASE... HELP!!!"

A few curious heads poke out of the main doorway, as I thunder past, my cape billowing behind me like a highly uncoordinated super-hero.

"THEY'VE GOT LARRY!!!" I yell into the room at no one in particular.

As I open the fire door, I'm vaguely aware of a surge of noise and activity behind me in the corridor. The landing before me is deserted. Heart-in-mouth I look at the flight that goes up.

No.

Somehow the voice of reason makes itself heard. They haven't had enough time to carry her up the stairs and out onto the roof.

And then a voice more powerful than reason starts talking...

Instinct.

The plan's changed. They're going to take her -

"Down there!" I scream, pointing at the descending staircase to the throng of people who have suddenly appeared right behind me.

Jess, the Irish soccer hooligans and a bunch of bar staff in lederhosen charge past me, heading full speed down the stairs. I follow them, with Rory at my side.

"The police are on the way..." he explains, as I clamber downwards as fast as my ridiculous heels will allow. I try to keep up with him, but I have no hope.

"Where does this go to...?" I try to yell to no one in particular, but my considerable lack of aerobic fitness is starting to be a problem.

"Street level..." Rory yells back up the stairs.

And somewhere in the back of my head, I hear the very calm voice of instinct again.

Carrying her body slowed them down too much... couldn't risk getting caught... they had to save themselves... so they abandoned Larry -

"She's here!" Jess' voice yells up from somewhere just below us, as several more flights down we hear a heavy door *bang!* as it slams shut.

And we round the corner... and at the bottom of the flight of stairs... surrounded by what should be a comical collection of concerned citizens... is the seemingly lifeless body of a life-size mermaid.

"*Larry!*" not yelling this time.

Rather a barely audible, choked gasp.

My heart feels like it's being squeezed in a vice as I consider a terrifying possibility. Larry is dead.

"It's okay. She's breathing. Are you okay...?" Rory asks. He sounds relieved as he slides an arm around me, squeezing hard to reassure me. "Jesus Kitty... I didn't expect the Knight in Shining Armour offer to be taken literally..."

I think I just blink, whilst alternately nodding and shaking my head.

What the fuck just happened...?

And what very nearly almost happened???

Jess is crouching over her, calmly checking vitals and airways, before carefully rolling her into the recovery position. She glances up at the surrounding crowd.

"I need a jacket or something - she's freezing cold."

Like Déjà Vu All Over Again...

So... for the second night in a row, I find myself riding in an ambulance... fielding a barrage of questions from paramedics, then ER nurses and doctors, then police constables...

Except this time, every interaction begins with raised eyebrows and "Nice dress!"...

To finally end up once again watching over a sleeping body from a highly inhospitable vinyl armchair.

Like Simon the night before, Larry was drugged with GHB. She's going to be okay.

Physically, that is.

Psychologically... who knows? Even for someone as spunky as Larry, it's a lot to deal with.

I'm feeling deeply rattled and I only watched it unfold...

And what is most disturbing is the entirely new angle that's presenting itself...

Consider Simon and Larry weren't just random victims of 'a lot of GHB on the streets'...? Consider someone was shooting for Larry last night and hit Simon by mistake...? Not unreasonable to assume the cocktail is for the pretty girl, is it…? Was Skeletor targeting Larry…? And who is Skeletor, anyway…???

My exhausted head keeps going round and round the same loop.

My nerves are cooked and my body feels like it's been hit by a freight train.

Oh… and let's not forget my poor feet! Right now I never want to walk again…

Then I have the unpleasant realisation that there's something I probably should attend to…

After a few minutes of agonised debate, I call the parents. The rationale being the only thing worse than telling TBJ her baby daughter has been drugged would be having to explain why I *hadn't* told her.

Thanks to her menopausal insomnia, TBJ answers the call instantly… then asks a barrage of increasingly focussed questions. Then hangs up to drag Dad out of bed to make the drive from Verity Park to the hospital.

I look down on Larry, and my heart trembles.

She looks angelic, like a princess in a fairytale, still in her sparkly mermaid dress with her pink ombré hair cascading over the white pillow. Her breathing soft and steady. Her face serene and beautiful.

What is going on...???

The police did not seem especially interested in my information about Skeletor or my theory that it was not coincidental. They basically blew me off.

But Gran told me to trust my instincts.

My instincts are telling me I'm missing something...

Important.

I really need to talk this through with somebody...

I really need to talk to Action Man.

Where the hell did that come from???

I'm clearly delirious because he's the last person on earth I want to be calling...

Clearly there's only one thing to do while I wait for Dad and TBJ to arrive... desperate times, desperate measures etc.

"Love you like a rainbow..." I murmur softly under my breath. The words catch on the unexpected lump that's suddenly in my throat.

Yes. She's a pain in the ass... but she's *my* pain in the ass. I gently smooth the inhospitable white hospital sheet, before dragging my exhausted, overwhelmed and traumatised body off in search of Maltesers...

I text Simon a quick update on Larry's progress as I get into the lift.

And he texts back that we won!

We were *all* winners - Best Group, Best Duet and Best Female.

Then he asks if I need a ride home, to which I'm replying I'll probably get one with my parents, when the elevator doors slide open and I hear...

"Nice dress!"

I look up into familiar grey eyes, a raised eyebrow and lips not even trying not to smirk. He's wearing scrubs and it looks like he's in the middle of a very long night.

"Oh God... *You* again...?"

Seriously I do not know what the odds are, but they are apparently *not* in my favour.

266

"I'm the one who gets paid to be here, Babe. You, however…?" he counters. His voice sounds tired, but he can still manage a fair hit of smugness.

"My sister's drink was spiked." I explain in a tired, quiet little voice.

"One friend getting roofied, Miss Carlisle, may be regarded as a misfortune. Two looks like carelessness…" he can't help but be impressed by his own cleverness for paraphrasing Oscar Wilde.

I reply with an eye roll.

"You don't have to go to all this trouble if you want to see me…. You could just call…"

"Fuck off…" I know. Sadly lacking in imagination, but after the crazy rollercoaster I've just been on, it's seriously the best I can do.

"Oh! So if anyone suggests Factitious Disorder Imposed on Another, I'll just recommend you for psychotherapy then…" he smirks quietly.

"*What?*" For once, I'm in no fit state to keep up with his cerebral gymnastics.

"Used to be Munchausen By Proxy… hurting people to get attention…?" he sighs and shakes his head. Sparring isn't much fun without a worthy adversary. So, following me to the vending machine, he changes tack. "What's with the dress…? Are you wearing that to win a bet…?"

"Eurovision." I explain. Like it is the only logical reason in the world.

"Oh I love Eurovision! Macedonia is always a really hot chick…" he enthuses, with a knowing, kinda sleazy nod.

I sigh and give him an eye-roll.

So predictable…

He hovers as I pull the roll of notes from my sleeve, and I'm just about to ask him if he doesn't have anything better to do, when I have a catastrophic realisation.

Vending Machines don't take hundred dollar bills.

I'm muttering a very passionate expletive, Jamie is staring in astonishment at my impressive collection of notes and asking if I have a Sugar Daddy, when…

Clunk! Clunk! Clunk! coins are deposited and a deep, Slavic accent asks…

"Whaddya want..?"

I look up to see Ivan, wearing a black designer tracksuit and matching trainers. I tell him Maltesers, please.

"Excellent choice! Hey - nice dress!" He's the only person so far tonight to say this without irony...

"Eurovision Party..." I explain, and thank him for the shiny little red bag of yumminess.

"Oh! How did Croatia do...? Most excellent song... and very handsome Croatian man..." but he doesn't wait for the answer, instead beckoning me to follow him. "Come! Boss wants to see you. Now."

"Nice dress!" Sebastian Marchesi grins at me from his hospital bed.

He looks in better shape than he did last night, but seeing him in a hospital gown and hooked up to beeping, blinking machines with tubes and wires...there's something disturbingly... uncharacteristically... vulnerable about him. Nero gets to his feet and gingerly poking the very short hemline with his nose, stares up at me with one raised tan eyebrow.

Yes. Even the dog is taking the piss out of my dress.

"Eurovision Party." I reply, for what seems like the hundredth time tonight. With ridiculous heels and micro dress, I awkwardly bend down to give Nero a pat. "And the host was Germany! You shoulda been there!"

"Now... I know I asked to meet with you *early as possible* this morning..." as he glances idly at his very expensive watch, "however I wasn't expecting you to interpret that literally..."

I can see from the hands on his platinum Rolex that we're barely a few minutes into tomorrow. My brain involuntarily calculates how many hours until I have to be at work... and it's not pretty.

"My sister had her drink spiked." I explain.

"Mmmm... lot of GHB on the street right now..." Ivan nods knowingly.

So people keep sayin'...

"However it would appear Miss Carlisle's friends seem to be disproportionately unlucky..." Sebastian frowns slightly, before changing the subject. Back to Himself. He fishes two envelopes from the drawer next to his bed.

One addressed to Holly. The other is blank. And it will be filled with hundred dollar bills.

"You're *a tad* earlier than anticipated, however... Sveta will deliver a pair of vases and a chicken to Le Jardin after school drop off..."

270

"Oh you were serious about the chicken! I thought you were delirious..."

"The chicken is of the utmost importance!" he replies, almost perfectly seriously but for a cheeky glimmer in his eye. "Do something very special and pretty in the vases - oh! They're quite valuable, so please handle with care-"

Oh God! I wish he hadn't told me that...

"- and, as usual, please be in and out of the penthouse before 10.30..." as he hands over the two envelopes, his face softens. "Thank you, Cressida. It's always a pleasure to see you. And I hope your sister is okay."

"Thank you. Hey..."

I know this is possibly a mistake. But in defence I am *very* tired. And if you want to know the answer, why not just ask the question... right...?

"What happened...? On the beach road...? In your garage...? It wasn't just an accident, was it...?"

Ivan shoots a warning glance to Marchesi. Instantly on high alert. Seb dismisses his concern with a barely perceptible shake of his head.

"Show her." Marchesi quietly commands Ivan.

Fleetingly he frowns reluctantly, taps a few times on a tablet then shows me the screen.

CCTV footage.

A vast, immaculately landscaped circular driveway at night. A white mini van appears, closely followed by a blank, white semi-trailer attached to a Mack truck.

A small army of men in black pit suits, trainers and balaclavas get out.

Interior of a huge, high tech warehouse with a polished, white floor... and row upon row of cars.

Beautiful, remarkable and expensive-looking collectible cars.

Men in black target very specific cars. With military precision each one approaches their vehicle and unplugs something.

"What are they doing?" I ask.

"Disconnecting magnetic trickle chargers. Keeps the batteries healthy." Seb replies quietly as he stares impassively at the screen.

Then they open their respective driver's door, slide into the seat and wait.

Two more men in black approach a giant, fancy lock-box on the wall with some kind of power tool.

An angle grinder, maybe...?

"The key safe...?" I ask.

Seb and Ivan both nod, calm and emotionless.

A man approaches a camera. Then darkness. Over and over again until every camera is blind.

"But Sveta said nothing was stolen..." I frown.

"Nothing." Ivan shakes his head ever so slightly, his face expressionless. "Nothing stolen, nothing moved. No footprints. No tyre tracks."

"You were deep faked...?" I ask, wide eyed and incredulous.

"We were extremely deep faked. That had to be shot in my garage." Marchesi's voice is calm, but there's a steely, resolute note that makes the hairs on my arms stand on end.

"Couldn't they just fake the footage...?"

"Not possible. Those girls are rare on the world market, let alone here-"

"Not faked. Expert go through it frame by frame. Very real... *very professional...*" Ivan's voice trails off. The fact that he is so calm makes him somehow even more menacing.

"They knew every security measure in place."

"Man... you were deep faked!" I know I'm repeating myself, but how often does the opportunity to use Deep Fake in perfect context come up in a conversation...?

But... we've done some big parties at his beach house... Huge marquees on the rolling lawn high on a cliff that overlooks the ocean. And underneath that lawn - James Bond style - is his giant car bunker.

He's techie, he's cautious-to-paranoid and money is no object. The security would be state of the art. And what about the-

"Where were your staff???" I blurt out.

"My live-in garage manager is in Darwin for his daughter's wedding... The last time he was away was Christmas... *Someone's* playing a long game..."

"Do you think he had anything to do with it?"

"God no!" Seb replies instantly and with passion. "He's one of my oldest friends. He had a few bad breaks in business... he's a bigger car nerd than me, so he was perfect for the role, and I was glad I could help him out. He has my back."

"*Someone* went to a lot of trouble to put you on that road last night... where you have a potentially fatal *random accident*...?" I frown. "It would appear my friends aren't the only *disproportionately unlucky* ones..."

Marchesi is carefully contemplating his reply when his phone rings. His eyes narrow, but the corners off his mouth turn up slightly.

"Shouldn't you be asleep...?" he asks, trying to sound stern but failing miserably. "You're back at school tomorrow... Do at least try not to get yourself suspended - I feel like I'm systematically refurbishing that school... one building and amenity at a time..."

Ah! The Mini Me. He says something that receives a curt, dismissive laugh.

"You think I won't be able to beat you one handed...?" he asks incredulously. "Sveta tried to smuggle a console in so I could get in some practice, but a highly officious nurse confiscated it... Anyway, I'll be home tomorrow... Oh I don't know if I'm being discharged, but I'm not spending another day in here. I'm going stir crazy."

He listens to Max with a smile and a partially raised eyebrow. It's very clear neither of them has any intention of sleeping any time soon. He looks so happy, relaxed, entertained and proud that I suddenly feel like I'm intruding.

Catching his eye, I motion to the door with a little nod of my head. Mouthing *Good Night!*, with a little wave I slip out into the corridor.

Leaving TBJ to watch over Larry, Dad comes down with me to wait for my Uber.

"Nice dress!" he smirks. "Your mother had one just like it in cobalt blue in the 80's..."

"I will have you know *I won!* Best Costume. 250 bucks!"

"Hmmm..." he nods, impressed. "250 bucks is 250 bucks!"

"That's what I said!"

Oh hang on... that was Gr-ah-nt.

It's 1am, and after way too many hours in these ridiculous heels, my feet are literally howling at me. The struggle is real and I'm barely winning the battle to put one foot in front of the other.

"I've seen new-born calves better on their legs..." Dad chuckles softly as he slides an arm around my waist, trying to help me.

I'm so exhausted, I don't know if I'm running on auto-pilot or just plain delirious.

As my car pulls up, I thank Dad, and with a hug and a kiss Good Night, slump onto the back seat like a broken doll.

"Nice dress!" jokes the angsty middle-aged white man behind the wheel.

Oh great!

Conspiracy Pete.

"Eurovision Party," is now my conditioned response.

And if I thought the dog dissing my dress was low, I am now having the piss taken by an overweight, balding man in a 'hilarious' novelty science hoodie (*Quantum physics is neither here nor there...* Tee hee, right?)

"Eurovision?!" he snaps, suddenly triggered. "You know what's *really* going on, don't you...?"

"It's rigged. Politically allied countries always vote for each other...?" is my bored and exhausted response.

"*Obviously!*" Pete splutters with disdain.

"Rich countries buy their votes...?"

"Yesyesyes..." he mutters, shaking his head violently.

"Every third year the People's Choice wins...?"

"Really?" for a split second, he's interested. Then the voices in his head regain control. "*No!* It's all about the messages in the songs!"

"What...? Peace, love... and trying not to invade each other...?"

"*NO!!!*" he almost yells, becoming more agitated by the second. "The messages when you play the songs backwards. You know who they're from...?"

"The aliens...?" To be fair, Pete, this answer is usually a pretty safe bet.

"Aliens???" he replies incredulously. Yes. Conspiracy Pete is now looking at me like I'm the crazy one. "No... no! *They're messages from Elvis!* Obviously..."

Fortunately I'm saved from (once again) hearing Pete's (very detailed and elaborate) version of events pertaining to Elvis faking his own death, by the abrupt arrival of the car at my apartment building.

After hauling my poor broken body up what feels like a million stairs, I collapse next to the very wide awake looking Simon and Danh on the velvet couch.

I fill them in as Simon gently pulls off the offending boots for me… left foot… right foot… and Danh removes what feels like a million bobby pins from my head.

In my room, I wriggle out of the sparkly purple Nice Dress and let it fall to the floor while I set an alarm on my phone.

Not even five hours… I tell myself as I slip into the groovy black wrought iron bed Simon and I dragged home from somebody's nature strip during a Council hard rubbish collection.

You need to sleep.

Now!

But there's something I need to figure out…

Even though my brain is melted and fuzzy… and the wheels are turning so, so slowly… there's something here that really doesn't make sense… but I just know somewhere in there, I know the answer…

What is it…? What is it…?

And just as I doze off, I have a glorious moment of clarity.

The stairs.

Going up.

Why would I think they would go up…?

Why would they want to go up? Wouldn't they just want to get her out of there...?

Then I see her body... falling past the window...

They were going up the stairs...

Because they didn't want to abduct her.

They wanted to push her off the roof.

And make it look like an accident.

Yeah... that's it...

An accident...

An unobtrusive dark figure slips down a dimly-lit, deserted service corridor. They carry a caddy of cleaning supplies in one hand and a full garbage bag in the other. Calm. Confident. Purposeful.

Coming to a halt in front of an unremarkable door, a black-gloved hand enters a security code into a key pad without missing a beat. With a soft click, the locking mechanism releases and the figure slips through the doorway.

Darkness. The garbage bag is placed on the ground, freeing up a hand to produce a tiny torch.

The pin-like beam of light offers so little illumination, it's basically useless.

Unless you know exactly where you're going.

The figure turns into what feels like a small room and places the torch and the caddy on a narrow white bed. A black-gloved hand carefully positions the torch and a white plastic console with a screen and a bunch of white spiral cables appears.

Deftly the black-gloved hands go to work.

Screwdriver. Tiny wire cutters. Needle-nose pliers. And...

What is that???

A turned-wood handle. Well-used, but very well looked after. With a metal head, the size of a razor blade. With irregular teeth and tiny, irregular sized holes...

But before I can wonder any more, the figure demonstrates its use. With machine-like efficiency, it strips red wires and black wires of their plastic coating.

A small part is removed from the machine, and replaced with one from the caddy.

In a matter of seconds, everything appears precisely as it was... and the figure is slipping down the darkened corridor to the exit... picking up the garbage bag and vanishing.

Either unperturbed or oblivious to the faint alarm that's just started bleeting...

The figure reappears... but now we're somewhere cold, dark and cavernous... Barely pausing to pick the lock, the handle turns and a big, metal cabinet door swings open.

Would someone please turn off that freaking alarm...??? It sounds like it's still a long way away, but undeniably it's gets insistently, persistently louder...

The figure pauses thoughtfully, familiarising themself with the rows of wires and circuits. As the alarm becomes almost intolerable, the figure steps into an abyss.

Freefalling.

And just as it all fades to black, one thing suddenly becomes very clear.

It's an elevator shaft.

Getting one's wires crossed...

The bliss of my warm, soft, dark little world is interrupted from seemingly a very long way away by a very irritating noise.

Sleepily I roll over, in the hope it will go away.

However it only gets closer.

Louder. More insistent.

And I have to face two terrible realisations.

One... we have unfortunately arrived at Monday Morning and I have about forty minutes before I need to be starting work.

And Two... I'm pretty sure I've just seen a ninja messing with electrical medical equipment and an elevator.

Which can only mean they're trying again to take out Marchesi, right...?

Unsteady and a little dizzy, I throw myself through the shower. Too many nights of drama and not enough sleep, with the added complication of a psychic nightmare... or two... I really hope my hair is okay because I don't have the time or motivation to wash it.

I pull on a pair of my more presentable jeans, a cute camel sweater with tweed elbow patches and a moss-green puffer vest. I grab some cosy, fluffy socks and gently ease my poor, passive-aggressive feet (that are still not speaking to me after last night...) into my tan Adidas sneakers.

Simon and Danh are sitting on the couch catching up on their Socials, looking smooth, polished and professional. How they manage to be so together on so little sleep is life's greatest mystery.

"You drink the blood of small children, right...?" I ask them, husky and exhausted.

"You need a ride to work, right...?" asks Simon with a raised eyebrow as he hands me a piece of toast and a warm sippy cup that I'm praying is full of coffee.

The concrete bunker is filled with grim, tired faces for whom one day off after Bo Day and M Day was clearly not nearly enough - except for Troy, who's apparently drinking the blood of young children too, looking tall, tanned and fabulous as ever. That he's nearly completed a full length casket topper would suggest that he started work when most of us were still asleep. On my work station, there's a pile of orders for Seb Marchesi prioritised in order of importance of client.

Without looking up from the beautifully blown spray of iceberg roses he's trying to wiggle into the oasis foam base, Troy starts…

"Right! Kitty-Kat! This is for a 9am funeral service at Drummond's… the top three orders for Sebastian Marchesi *must* be delivered to the hospital this morning - one's from Bruno Mancini - the rest can wait til he goes home… So… drop *this* off on the way to the hospital, get back here to do some orders for the 12 pickup, then go to Casa Marchesi and check with the Boa if she wants any more flowers and refurb anything that's looking sad…"

Hope there's not much else required of me, because looks like I'm fully occupied with my favourite mogul for the day…

So… after smashing out a few orders and the Big Three for Mr M, I brave peak hour traffic to get the casket flowers to Drummond's Funeral Parlour in time for their last goodbye… then head across to St. Francis'.

As the lift doors open onto the sixth floor, I hold my breath... but no! For once, the coast is clear and there's no Dr Wolfe waiting to pounce.

Approaching Marchesi's room, I can faintly hear raised voices. Sebastian and Bo Marchesi.

And then I get close enough for the words to become clear...

Waiting in the corridor, Ivan is scrolling through his phone and Nero is staring at an invisible mark on the floor, both feigning deafness to the escalating slanging match in the room.

"This has been discussed!" Seb's voice is fighting to remain calm. "Ava is not going to Paris. She'll miss too much school."

"*School...?*" The Boa hisses disdainfully. "Who gives a fuck about *school...?* We can be famous!"

"This is all about you, isn't it?! Using your daughter to try to make yourself relevant... It's tragic, Bo." Seb begins quietly incredulous... and ends cruelly dismissive.

"I'm not losing momentum! That Vogue cover will launch her international career-" The Boa shrieks back, her cultivated accent slipping and a harsh, ugly tone taking its place - leaving no doubt that it *is* indeed all about her...

"*SHE'S NOT GOING!*" Marchesi roars at his wife.

For a rare moment, he is terrifyingly... compellingly... out of control. The heart rate monitor starts beeping loudly.

"Yes. She is. I've made all the arrangements." The Boa counters. Spitefully, calmly and matter-of-factly.

"I will flag her passport at emigration if I have to..." Marchesi replies, equally calmly and matter-of-factly.

"You wouldn't dare! Ava is going to Paris! What kind of father kills his daughter's dreams???" The Boa spits back, her voice dripping with hatred.

"They're not Ava's dreams... *they're your dreams!*" he roars back at her.

"*We are going to Paris!*" Bo is screaming at him.

"Over my dead body!" Marchesi snaps back at her.

"*That* can be arranged..." Bo's eyes narrow to tiny slits as she hisses like a viper.

Unlike Ivan and Nero, I'm not great at pretending to be deaf. I really don't want to hear any more, and the very large box filled with three carefully packed VIP Get Well Soon flower arrangements is getting heavier and heavier by the minute.

I take a deep breath and knock hard as I can on the door before pushing it open.

They both freeze, eying each other suspiciously like fighting dogs that have been pulled apart.

Bo recovers first, clearing her throat and locating her smooth, posh gazillionaire wife voice.

"Must run, Darling. Manicure at 10, then my Monday facial with Holly at 11..."

If you weren't looking for it, you wouldn't see Marchesi's jaw clench ever so slightly at the mention of Holly's name.

"Do you know when they're sending you home...?" Bo tries very hard to keep her voice light and casual, but for a fleeting second her spectacular aquamarine eyes are stone cold and calculating.

"They still won't tell me anything..." Marchesi replies smoothly and evasively. And just as I'm thinking how impressive his Poker Face is, he doubles down. "Say Hi to Holly for me - and tell her I'll be fine to see her for my appointment on Thursday night."

After she leaves, he stares at me for a moment. Impassively.

"I'm sorry you had to hear that," he apologies quietly. Then with a little self-deprecating snort continues. "I'm sorry anyone had to hear that..."

I start placing the moderately sized but very expensive arrangements on empty, flat surfaces, unpinning the cards from the luxe, handsome bows and handing them to Marchesi.

"This is from Bruno Mancini... this is from your CEO... and this is from the Premier's office..." I raise an impressed eyebrow as I say it.

Languidly he casts his eyes over the cards, chuckling at whatever Bruno Mancini has scribbled in Italian. I know I have to get moving - I have so much stuff to do for him today I'm almost wondering who I work for - but there's one thing that's been bugging me.

"Do you think they'll try again...?" I ask. Quietly but assertively.

"I would." He replies completely without guile. Or filter.

"Be careful..." I pause. I don't really know how to say this, but I know I won't forgive myself if I don't... "Be careful of any different electrical equipment... And be careful in lifts..."

"You're starting to sound like Ivan..." he half-smiles, mockingly, at me.

"When you go home...?" I ask, with a heavy Croatian accent. Exactly like Ivan.

He smiles.

"This afternoon. Before the kids come home from school. But that's Top Secret. Nobody else knows."

I've no idea why he tells me his secrets. It makes me feel privileged... and uncomfortable.

In equal measures.

Waiting for the elevator and hoping I can once again be fortunate enough to not encounter any Wolves on the prowl, I shoot off a quick text.

ME How r u???

LARRY Fine
Errrr... how r u?

ME I didn't get roofied & kidnapped last night!
Seriously - you ok?

LARRY So people keep sayin'

Have no recollection at all

& THX for sending TBJ - NOT!!!

Gotta go - HOT DOCTOR!!!

Shaking my head, I step into the lift.

But of course!

Never let the inconvenience of potentially dying get in the way of a Flirting Opportunity...

Welcome to Planet Larry!

There's a thunk and a rattle from the back of the van as I hit the speed hump going into the Marquis underground carpark a little too fast. Wincing, I remember too late the two very valuable vases on board. I'm supposed to have this delivery done before 10.30.

I'm cutting it very, very close.

I grab the gigantic box and hustle to the discreet penthouse lift. I key in the code, and the doors slide open.

I jump in and hastily push the Up button.

After a few minutes of nothing happening - which is most unusual and *hey!* I don't have a few minutes to waste right now - I thump the Up button repeatedly.

Impatiently.

But instead of going up, the doors slide smoothly open.

And just as I'm about to start belting the Close Doors button, I notice a figure standing there.

Tallish and slim. Glossy dark hair with a thick, blunt fringe and jaunty ponytail. Oversize dark tortoiseshell Jackie O sunglasses, violet puffer jacket, black yoga pants, white sneakers. Holding a very large takeaway coffee.

Meet Holly.

We stare at each other.

Awkward and uncomfortable.

So *this* is why I had to be out of here by 10.30... and because I was running late, I've officially let Seb's top secret cat out of the bag.

Frozen in awkwardness, we just stand there staring at each other in overly-polite silence.

Awkward on many levels. I'm not supposed to know who she is - *Nobody* is supposed to know who she is, because this is a social and political tinder box. With the added complication that as well as

being beauty magician to the rich and famous, Holly recently became *my* beauty therapist... so I not only know who she is, I actually
know her personally and professionally.

And I'm not sure if that makes it better or worse...

Then Holly diffuses it all with a laugh.

A charming, musical, child-like laugh as she steps purposefully
into the lift, pushing up her sunglasses so they sit between her fringe
and pony like a headband.

"I believe all that's for me!" she declares quietly, with a sweet,
shy smile. "I can take it up for you, if you're in a hurry..."

"It's fine, thank you..." I very politely decline. "I have very specific instructions."

"Oh I'm sure you do!" she replies with a theatrical eye roll. Then
she suddenly becomes very earnest. "Have you seen him today? Is
he okay? When are they letting him go home...?"

I answer her questions as best I can while she presses the Up
button.

"This is killing me. I've been so worried about him..." she almost
whispers as we begin our ascent.

But suddenly we grind to a halt.

We exchange a frown, then Holly taps the Up button briskly.

But nothing happens.

She tries again. Harder. Repeatedly. As concern starts sliding into panic.

"No. No. No. No." She mutters, her glossy buffed natural nails hitting the Up button over and over.

But we're still not moving.

"This cannot happen! I have Bo Marchesi at 11..."

"Can you call somebody?" I ask hopefully.

"There's no phone reception in here..." Holly wails. "Shit! Shit! Shit!"

She punctuates each expletive with a frustrated *bang!* on the Up button. And then, simultaneously, our eyes fall on the cleverly concealed mirrored panel and finally logic kicks in.

Her fingers fumble for a few seconds, then it smoothly pops open... to reveal a button with a red phone symbol and an intercom.

Holly presses the button, but before she can speak, a smooth, professional female voice takes charge.

"Good morning Miss Cabanel... There seems to be a problem with the electrics. We'll have someone there within the hour-"

294

"I don't have an hour! I have to be somewhere-" and while po-lite-and-nice is Holly's default setting, I can see her starting to spiral.

"Is there someone I can call for you?"

Holly flicks frantically through her contacts, then offers up a name and number.

"It's urgent. Please explain my situation, then tell her I need her to look after Bo Marchesi at 11. It's a galvanic current facial - the notes are on her file." Holly instructs the Voice quickly, clearly and emphatically.

"On it! Will confirm soon as it's done. Please press the call button to answer."

And abruptly the line goes dead.

Holly stands, staring at the intercom with her hand anxiously on her lips and her dark blue eyes in a world of pain. I cannot even imagine what it must be like for her... It's bad enough when The Boa is just ruining your professional life, let alone inadvertently ruining your private life too.

"I thought the salon was closed on Mondays..."

"Oh, it is. Unless you're *her* and you refuse to share the facility with any other client…" Even sweet, lovely Holly can't keep the bitterness from her voice. "I have to do two hours of pilates before her appointment just so I don't strangle her."

"What's a galvanic facial?" I'm not particularly interested, but from the look on Holly's face, I feel a change of subject could be helpful.

"We use low voltage electrical currents to stimulate cellular repair, improve circulation and facilitate product absorption." She explains, sounding quite grateful to be distracted by something that's in her wheel house.

"Electric current…?" I frown, possibly looking somewhat alarmed.

"Oh it's perfectly safe and painless. The client holds an electrode, which allows the body to conduct a current when metal rollers are applied to the face. It's also used in injury rehab-"

Holly's increasingly enthusiastic infomercial is cut short by the intercom buzzing.

Holly cannot hit the button fast enough.

"Miss Cabanel? Just letting you know Claudia is fine to fill in for you and estimates she will be at the salon at 10.55am."

"Oh thank God!" Holly's relief is palpable.

"And a technician should be on site within thirty minutes. Is there anything else I can assist with?"

I ask the Voice to call Troy and explain my unavoidable detainment... which he's *really* not going to like on a Monday...

Holly suddenly frowns.

"Can you smell roast chicken...?"

I gesture down to the very large box in my arms... the very large box that is becoming increasingly heavy.

In between two exquisitely delicate pink arrangements, in exquisitely (expensively) delicate palest green Chinese vases decorated with hand-painted pink peonies... is an elaborate glass cloche tied onto a serving platter with an elaborate pink taffeta bow... under which is a glorious, golden brown roast chicken.

She shakes her head, laughing.

"I can't believe he made Sveta cook me a chicken!"

"He was most adamant about the chicken - at first I thought it was the concussion talking..." I giggle.

"I keep telling him I don't need *stuff*... but he's not going to stop, is he...?"

"Every Monday he *agonises* over what to send you..." I tell her, with a conspiratorially raised eyebrow. And then before I can stop it, it comes out of my mouth. Quietly and seriously. "You make him so happy."

"I think he's the most remarkable man I've ever met. I adore him." She replies softly, straight from the heart.

And because it's suddenly awkwardly apparent that we've both said too much, Holly abruptly changes the subject.

"Hey! That looks heavy. Let me help you put it down..." as she gracefully commandeers one end of the giant box, helping me place it on the floor.

Without even thinking, she is so thoughtful, kind and sweet. It's her first instinct. It's no wonder her day spa is so successful... it's so natural for her to take care of people. It's actually not possible for her to be more *unlike* Bo Marchesi...

"Do you think they're actual Qing dynasty vases...?" she asks warily, admiring the delicate hand-painted collars barely visible from the newspaper packing.

"He did warn me to be careful with them..." I reply hesitantly. Generally, my track record with fragile isn't too bad, but I'll be very happy to hand them over and make them Holly's problem.

She raises her perfect eyebrows and makes a charmingly goofy *Eeeek!* face.

"So... what have you got on for the rest of the day?" she asks thoughtfully.

"I have to catch the bullet you dodged..." I grimace. "Marchesi House flowers... check on her birthday flowers... and try to discuss what she wants to do with all the orders for Mr M..."

Can't help it. Just the thought of having to be in the same room with her makes me shudder.

"Don't for one second think I've dodged the bullet..." she laughs, not without irony. "Do you seriously think she's going to be happy about Claudia treating her...?"

"Oh God no! Seriously, how do we put up with her???" I ask the question, which I'm painfully aware is rhetorical. When you have that much money, people *have* to put up with you.

"You know what helps me...?" she asks with a sly grin and a sneaky raised eyebrow. "You know what Sveta does to get her back...?"

"Shrinks her clothes so she thinks she's getting fat...? Secretly gives her weight gain shakes...?"

"Oh... so, so much worse!" Holly's pretty face lights up with glee. "She cleans toilets with Bo's very expensive ultrasonic toothbrush!"

And as we stare at each other, partners in crime, a tiny bit horrified but mostly revelling in the guilty pleasure of Schadenfreude, the elevator gives a jolt before smoothly resuming it's ascent to the penthouse.

"The truth is rarely pure and never simple..." Oscar Wilde

Trying to convince Troy that I had, indeed, been stuck in a lift for an hour was a bit like trying to convince the teacher that the dog really *did* eat your homework... and I couldn't really ask Holly to corroborate, could I?

I smash out a few orders while scoffing down a glorious, oozy, buttery toasted ham, cheese and avo sandwich from Hangry - the little cafe at the end of the laneway that we pretty much keep in business.

Just as I'm contemplating whether my tired and emotional state could be improved with a hot chocolate, Troy says those dreaded words - *You better get yourself to the Marchesi house... Now!*

After rolling up the long, private driveway, Casa Marchesi finally appears.... with an ambulance blocking the front steps, completely obscuring the view of the front door. With a squad car parked right behind it.

I smile to myself. Looks like Mr M got himself a ride home... with a police escort.

In my dark green Le Jardin van, I follow the driveway around to the rear of the house unobserved. I knock on the service door, calling out to Sveta as I open it. Expecting her to instantly appear like a ninja, like she always does...

But the mud room is deserted...

The kitchen is deserted. The butler's pantry is deserted.

Where is everybody...?

I wander through the house... looking, listening for signs of life. Vaguely I'm aware of tyres on the gravel driveway and a series of car doors slamming shut.

I slip my dark green Le Jardin apron over my head and wrap the ties around my waist a couple of times before knotting them on my hip, as I head towards the front of the house. I hear voices coming from the formal sitting room. One is Sveta. The other a quietly authoritative female voice I don't recognise.

"Can you account for your whereabouts today?"

"Sorry...? My English not so good..."

I frown. Who's that...? And why Sveta is suddenly playing Dumb Foreign Housekeeper... her English is perfectly satisfactory.

"When did you last see Mrs Marchesi?" she asks.

"Last night. 8pm. I take her pills to her in bed."

"You didn't see her at all today?"

"No. I wake up kids, make lunch, cook breakfast, do school drop off. When I get home she gone. She visit Mr M in hospital. It's Monday so she have manicure at 10am and facial at 11am. Facial take one hour, she home ten minutes later."

"But you weren't here? Where were you?"

"I leave at ten to do shopping. I order cake for Mr M - he come home today - but cake not ready. Have to wait... I have coffee... Check! They see me there! I get home 12.35 maybe...? And first thing I see..."

Sveta falls silent.

The voice softens a little.

"I'm sorry Svetlana, but I need you to tell me what you saw."

"I see Mrs M. Lying on steps. Not moving. I call her name. Nothing! I try to feel pulse. Nothing! I call ambulance..."

What the fuck...???

A purposeful male voice jumps in.

"You mentioned pills? Where does Mrs Marchesi keep them? We'll need to have a look at them."

"This take much longer...? I need to speak to Mr M! We need to get kids home. Mr M needs to be here... he needs to tell them- He knows, right???"

"Yes. They sent somebody into the hospital."

Does he know what??? What does he need to tell the kids? What the hell is going on???

The front door opens and people in medium-pay-grade conservative suits appear. They don't look happy to see me.

"Who are you?" asks a particularly abrasive looking woman.

"I'm Cressida Carlisle from Le Jardin. I'm here to do the house flowers."

"How long have you been here...?" she asks with a suspicious frown.

I explain that I saw the ambulance when I drove in and assumed it was Mr Marchesi coming home.

"Miss Carlisle, I'm going to have to ask you to leave. You can't be here right now." She speaks with officious hostility as she shows me her police badge.

"What happened?" I ask, searching everyone's faces looking for a clue. I've become accustomed to having the psychic heads up, it feels odd to not already know...

But this time, there was no spoiler alert...

Was there...???

The cops shoot slightly irritated glances at each other before a young, more personable-looking guy replies...

"The housekeeper came home and found Mrs Marchesi lying on the front steps." And before I can ask any more questions, Sveta emerges with two uniform cops.

"Can you show us Mrs Marchesi's medication, please?" the guy asks, silently motioning at one of the female suits to follow them.

Sveta nods anxiously.

"I call you when it's okay to come back... Okay...?" she murmurs to me as she passes, gently clasping my arm reassuringly on the way through.

Fortunately, the butler's pantry is on the way out, so I follow behind them. Trying to overhear any snippet... trying to find any clues as to what the hell is going on.

Sveta indicates to one of the high cupboards, and the policeman opens the cabinet door. He whistles softly under his breath as he clocks the contents of the tray.

The two uniforms exchange a guarded, knowing glance, while the suit pulls on a pair of latex gloves.

"How was she even alive...?" mutters the suit as she starts inspecting the bottles.

Did she just say alive in the past tense...???

"Jesus! Look at all the names and pharmacies! Doctor shopping... *somebody* had a problem..." he mutters, shaking his head.

"And all the herbal supplements...! Just cos they're 'natural' doesn't make 'em any less dangerous... and the side effects any less serious..." the suit exclaims, frowning at the labels.

"I try to tell her! No good! No good! She no listen..." Sveta shakes her head mournfully.

And as that window during which I can reasonably hover without looking suspicious closes, I head out to my van.

"Cressida!" Sveta is following me out the service door. "You forget knife! You leave here on Friday!"

I feel her slip something into my apron pocket.

I know I didn't, but I don't argue with her.

Instead I ask-

"What the hell is going on???"

"Dead!" Sveta exclaims matter-of-factly.

"What...? Who? How?" I ask bewildered.

If that's a joke, it's not funny.

"Mrs M... drop dead on front steps... Looks like you have big white funeral to do... can't say *when*... Medical examiner will need to establish cause of death... maybe coronial inquiry..." Sveta sounds like she's discussing what's for dinner. You will also note she has regained the ability to speak English...

I shake my head in disbelief.

Along with God knows how many other people, I've wished her dead many, many times. Be careful what you wish for, hey...?

"Now he can be with Holly..." she states calmly.

"I guess if anything good can come out of it, they're lucky they can finally be together...." I reason absently. Thinking out loud. Still trying to get my head around this.

"Luck would not have happened without misfortune's help..." replies Sveta, with an odd little smile.

I shoot her a sharp glance, frowning.

What is she trying to say...?

"Is just Russian proverb... Will be hard, but kids will get over it... Toxicology report will find cocktail of amphetamines and contraindicating natural remedies... and congenital heart condition. Galvanic current not a good idea, but she never disclosed it." Sveta sounds perfectly calm and matter of fact. She raises a sly eyebrow. "Who knew facial could be so dangerous...?"

We've arrived at the van. I pause as I open the door.

"Lucky Holly wasn't there today! She could have been implicated..."

"Da..." Sveta nods wisely. "Luck would not have happened without misfortune's help..."

And she turns to head back into the house.

And I'm left to climb into the big, green van and try to process everything that's just happened. Despite my mind continually circling back to Sveta...

Misfortune's help.

My phone starts ringing.

Unknown caller.

I answer in case it's a client.

First it sounds like someone is shrieking in agony.

Which is alarming, but then I realise it's someone singing... singing the bridge from *Creep* with terrifying enthusiasm... which is so much worse.

You are fucking joking!

"Hey Cressida! It's Gr-ah-ah-nt. Simon gave me your number..." there's that irritatingly positive voice I was kinda hoping I'd never have to hear again.

Thanks Simon!

Note to self to punch Simon next time I see him...

Without waiting for a reply, he continues.

"So... when are we getting the band back together to celebrate our big win...? We have 500 bucks to get through... Bummer you weren't there for the presentation... oh! And it was a huge bummer that you basically ruined the whole presentation..."

"Gr-ah-ah-nt... This isn't a good time for me. But I will say there is no *we*... there's you... and there's me... and we're not getting the band back together-"

"Playing hard to get! I love it! Good chat. Talk soon!"

And he hangs up.

Jesus! Talk about luck not happening without misfortune's help... that $500 bar tab is suddenly working out far too costly...

Starting the van, I look up and I notice the ambulance driving away.

Trying *not* to think about the Boa's dead body being in it, I put the transmission into gear. There's that glossy, fat, black raven stomping officiously around on the steps... just like he was on Friday...

One for sorrow...

He approaches the beautiful gardenia plant, which is still exactly where I left it yesterday.

Yesterday!

Good golly! How can that just have been yesterday...?

With his chunky, pointy beak, he seems to be examining something on the rim of the terracotta pot.

Something red.

Blood!

Bo hit her head when she collapsed...?

Before I can start hypothesising over what actually killed her... heart or head trauma... and trying to dismiss the grimly ironic thought that Sebastian Marchesi potentially just killed his wife with a Mothers Day present... I become aware that the lap sash of my seatbelt is massively uncomfortable... and I have no idea why this is suddenly the case.

Reaching into the pocket of my apron, my fingers hit a smooth wooden handle.

What the...?

I have no idea what that could be...

However as soon as I fish it out and take one look at it, my breath catches in my throat and my heart skips a beat.

I know exactly what it is...

A turned wooden handle. Well-used but very well looked after. With a metal head the size of a razor blade. With irregularly spaced teeth and irregular sized holes.

And my mind spirals as I realise two things.

Rather than *not* seeing any of this... I'd actually dreamt all of it.

And that luck did, indeed, not happen without misfortune's help.

COUNTING SHEEP

Cressida Carlisle Mystery Number 3...

What happens next...???

Let's find out, shall we?!

Friday 7.11am
Believing six impossible things before breakfast...

Grrrrgghhhh!

Yep. That's my stomach.

Yep. I'm starving, but sadly I'm going to have to ignore that rumbling belly for now. Because I've got some serious picking to do...

It's a glorious cool, crisp country morning, but when the sun gets higher in this cloudless, bright blue sky, it's going to warm right up. Which means I'm racing the clock to cut everything I need for today before the morning dew starts evaporating.

I've already been at it for well over an hour, starting just before dawn. And I've already picked *a lot*... but to transform that humungous shearing shed from rustic to fairytale wedding, it's going to take mountains of flowers.

Not to mention the chapel... the bride... and the five bridesmaids...

The garden is seriously mind blowing. Well-established and clearly well-loved by a passionate gardener. October is generally a pretty exciting time of year for flowers in Melbourne, but this year conditions have been perfect.

I'm facing the gorgeous predicament of being completely overwhelmed with options. Every corner I turn leaves me speechless as I'm confronted by yet another magnificent, rare and special specimen, to which Mother Nature has obligingly brought her A Game.

Mother of the bride has instructed Miranda that I can cut anything I want for the wedding.

"When she said *anything*, I seriously hope she meant that quite literally..." I mutter under my breath as I reach for a pruning saw and start collecting branches from a spectacular mauve rhododendron hedge.

Carefully I fill a wheel barrow, then like a kid in a candy store, peek around the lush foliage to see what my next volunteers from the garden might be.

OMFG! A gigantic dogwood tree. Covered with the most heavenly palest pink flowers, so delicate they quiver like butterflies. I can't get to it fast enough! I break into a run, and am so completely captivated by it, I'm oblivious to anything else.

Slowly I circle the trunk, looking up in wonder at the branches... instantly thinking of the exposed beams in the chapel ceiling and how this will be absolute perfection... and wondering if there's a really tall ladder somewhere... when I become aware of a voice.

And it's calling my name.

"Cressida? Cressida darling! Come and join us!"

It's an educated, loud and forthright Mum's voice.

Slowly I turn to see a vast, sandstone outdoor table surrounded by a very large family having breakfast in front of a beautiful bluestone homestead.

With an embarrassed shrug, I start walking over.

Tallish, fifty-something, with big, brown eyes, beautiful bone structure and expensively highlighted chestnut hair. Back in the day, she would have been a heart breaker. She wipes her hands on her floral, floaty kaftan before extending one to me in introduction.

"Cressida! Lovely to meet you! I'm the Mother of the Bride... Simone..." as she warmly shakes my hand. "Have you had breakfast...? I'm used to feeding an army, so there's always plenty... Come and meet the tribe!"

I'd really like to say that I really don't have time to stop right now, but Simone isn't giving me that option.

I give them a self-conscious wave.

Seven very attractive faces are looking expectantly at me, ranging from roughly my age right through to a couple of teenagers and a pre-teen in school uniforms. Simone introduces them in chronological order.

Madeleine... Charlotte... Christian... Georgia... Ella... Carli... Phoebe...

"We're missing one!" Simone laughs. "Number One son works in Melbourne. He said he'll be here for dinner, but we won't hold our breath..."

With an eye-roll, Christian mouths *Number One Son* in a pretty funny impersonation of his mother, then gives me a cheeky wink.

"The more you cut down, the less I'll have to prune later. So knock yourself out!"

"It's the most beautiful garden! Thank you! This wedding is going to be so special..." And even though it's potentially already too late, I feel the need to clarify. "It's okay to cut anything, right...?"

"Oh yes, dear. They look so pretty in the garden now, but they can live forever in Georgie's wedding photos... Coffee? Eggs? Toast?"

I'm directed to an empty chair and, like magic, a steaming coffee mug and a plate of scrambled eggs on toast appears. Realising resistance is useless, I sit and eat.

"I can't tell you how happy we are your sister bought next door! Her plans are so exciting! Rural economies are pretty fragile... she'll really make difference to this town." Simone speaks passionately. Straight from the heart.

She explains that Madeleine is interested in event planning, Charlotte is a beauty therapist, and Georgia is training to be a florist. It's the perfect opportunity for her girls...

I feel what I think is a dog brush against my legs under the table. Then I feel little hands on my knees, followed by a little body climbing into my lap.

A toddler with short, dark plaits and pretty eyes.

Wearing a Batman suit... and can I just say, she's owning it! She sticks out her tongue at me, before grabbing a handful of scrambled eggs... which she splatters all over my face.

"Oh Harry! *No!*" shrieks Madeleine, apparently the mother of the rogue toddler, leaping up to rescue me.

"Oh she's fine..." I giggle as I brush lumps of egg from my black tank top. "I'm going to be getting pretty dirty in the garden..."

As plates and mugs are emptied, we make some more polite small talk about the garden and the weather. And I know it's probably not the right moment, but something has been knocking in my brain since I woke up and I can no longer ignore it.

"Can I ask a question...?" I hold my breath.

Here we go...

"Of course, dear. How can we help you...?" is Simone's hospitable reply.

"Do the names Tara and Jason mean anything...?" I ask around the table.

The coffee mug falls from Simone's hand to smash on the blue-stone pavers. There's a clatter as someone's cutlery falls from their hand. Someone clears their throat awkwardly and everyone looks away or casts their eyes downwards.

"Oh clumsy me!" Simone recovers, brusquely. "Goodness! Is that the time? Must dash... Ella! Carli! Phoebes! In the car! We'll be late for school... Christian Charles! Can you clean up this mess please...? Last thing I need is having to take bleeding Barney to the vet..."

And suddenly everyone at the table has a very important date.

And without saying a word, they tell me exactly what I needed to know.

I inhale very slowly, as that increasingly familiar feeling of dread starts rising from my toes. Last night I didn't just have a hideous nightmare about two teenagers meeting a terrible end... I saw how Tara and Jason were killed...

And I know it's going to be up to me to find out who did it...